SUGAR CANE

by

Alex Morgan

LMH Publishing Limited

Alex Morgan

Cover design and illustrations by Susan Lee-Quee

Book design and typesetting by A.C. Lewinson-Morgan
Set in 12/16 Times New Roman x 25.5 / Freeform721 BT

Published by LMH Publishing Limited
7 Norman Road
LOJ Industrial Complex, Building 10
Kingston CSO, Jamaica WI
Tel: 876-938-0005; 938-0712
Fax: 876-928-8036

Email: lmhpublishing@cwjamaica.com
Website: www.lmhpublishingjamaica.com

Printed by Lightning Source Inc., USA   ISBN: 976-8184-086

For Jamie-Rai Morgan
You really scared us back there ... you really did.

Alex Morgan

Only Heaven Can Wait
by
Roberta Flack

Why do we stay together?
We can't wait forever,
Heaven's too late,
Only heaven can wait for love.

Prestigious Dogs
by
Sugar Cane

Why do you hate me?
Is it the clothes I wear?
The God I pray to?
Or the length of my hair?
The world is wide and
What must be has to be!
Prestigious dogs won't ever
Take control of me.

Alex Morgan

CHAPTER ONE

IT WAS dusk when they actually saw the new tenant. And it was only now that they discovered he was a Rastafarian. Paul Frater never once mentioned this part to them. Perhaps he thought it wasn't really necessary as the dreadlocks look was so much of a fad these days. Perhaps he was right. But then, perhaps he thought too damn much for his own good.

"Damn freak," Hector White went under his breath. He shifted uneasily in the Rubbermade chair. An uncomfortable feeling came over him as the man approached the veranda. Hector didn't outright hate Rastafarians but he didn't entirely adore them either. For one he thought they were just too naive to still think Selassie was indeed God. Then they also had the hope of one day going back to Africa to live. Africa! Now, considering Africa's present state, why would anyone in his right mind want to do that? But were these weed-smoking social rejects in their right minds? Maybe not, Hector thought, maybe not at all. Perhaps they had acquired a sort of madness which made them think they were African Lions; making them desire to grow their hair into manes and culture their odours till they smelled like horse shit. And

1

quite likely, he thought, it was that weed they smoked so copi-ously that gradually brought them to that state.

"Instead of a human being," Hector grumbled again, "Frater sends a beast to live under the same roof with me. What on earth! did I do to deserve this?"

"Hector, he might hear you," Sharon Gordon cautioned. She occupied the chair beside him.

"So what if he does hear me? Probably can't understand a damn thing I say anyway," Hector chuckled, his beer-gut bob-bing under the one-size-too-small T-shirt he had on. "Maybe he's so beastly he can't figure out a word of English anymore."

"Let's just assume he still can," Sharon suggested and crossed her legs. She dangled a slipper from her toes. Her annoyance wasn't only in her tone but clearly etched on her face too.

"Assume your ass!" he exclaimed, loud enough for the ap-proaching figure to hear. "That's what's wrong with you; you're afraid of sayin' what you truly feel. Hypocrite!"

She sighed. "You're so right."

"But of course. If a thing's a spade call it a spade. I'm not afraid to say that I hate livin' in a tenement house, and now that a rastaman's livin' here too only add wood to the fire."

"Okay, Hector, you've made your point," Sharon said realising the new tenant was now definitely too close for this conversation to continue.

"Greetin's," the man said as he climbed the last of three steps to the veranda. He had a guitar in a canvas case slung across his back, and his locks were all bundled up under the knitted, rain-bow coloured tam he wore. His smile was wide and he smelled of carbolic soap and not the horse shit Hector had been bracing himself for.

"You must be our new neighbour," Sharon said. Her smile, though quite genuine, was not as convincing as his. The bulky impression his locks made against the tam knit made her wonder just how long they were when let loose. Probably all the way down to the brink of his butt, she thought. There was something about a man who grew his hair that long that just fascinated her. It reminded her of Samson in the Bible: the strongest man who ever lived. In the five years they had been together, Sharon had never even mentioned this to Hector for she was too aware of how he detested this sect.

"Yes, sister," he said, "I an' I will be the man with the guitar in the back-room for a little while."

"Thought dreadlocks don't live in tenement yard," Hector went. He kept his gaze beyond the other man as if something out by Brown's Hall Crossroads had captured his interest. Actually, there was nothing there to see except Nissan Sunny cabs waiting for customers and a boy of about eleven going home, a bucket of drinking water perched on his head. This was quite the usual scene of Brown's Hall's centre on a Monday evening—or any other evening for that matter. It was the nightlife of a rural district: peaceful to the point of boredom.

"Hard times, brother," the rastaman said matter-of-factly, "hard times call for desperate measures, even for a Rasta."

"But you people chant to Selassie so much I thought him would save you all from the times."

"Brother," the dreadlocks said, "to tell you the truth, I an' I used to think so too."

3

This brought a chuckle out of Hector. It was a genuine one. "Selassie fuck you up!"

"Call it that," the dreadlocks said. This brought an even longer, louder chuckle from Hector. In fact, this was a full-blown laugh. And he thought of relating it to the boys if he got around to going by Tony's for a few beers tonight. He hated the shit the rastaman represented but he could make him laugh.

"But the true servant will keep the faith," the dread added on a more serious note. "Can't give up on the creator at all, brother."

"Sure," Hector went cynically.

"True," Sharon said, nodding her head in agreement with the Rastafarian.

"What you talkin' 'bout true like you in this Rasta thing with them?" Hector asked. He scratched at his day-old stubble.

"You don't have to be a Rasta to know that you should hold onto what you believe in."

"You sound like them," Hector told her with some amount of disgust.

"The sister sound like a philosopher," the rastaman stated, to Sharon's delight. "A sister like you could help me write my songs." He could see her blush uncontrollably when he said this.

Hector gave this one a good bar laugh. The first encounter with the beast was turning out more hilarious than he could ever have thought. "Sharon, help with songs? The man to produce that would be a damn jackass with a lot of money. Take my advice, baby, stick with nursin'."

Sharon ignored the remark. "So you're a songwriter?"

"Tryin' to be's more like it." He took the cased guitar into his hands. His gaze at the instrument reflected the magnitude of respect he had for it. "With the help of Jah, though, one day I'll become great at it. Maybe as great as Brother Bob Marley himself." The words were spoken with much passion, as if he had been struggling with the dream for years and simply refused to let it go.

"Any songs published yet?" Sharon asked, finding hypnotic interest in the man's voice.

"One," he answered with some degree of pride. "Ever heard a song call Prestigious Dogs?"

She thought, then shook her head slowly, still thinking.

"Radio stop playin' fart a long time ago," Hector grumbled. Neither Sharon nor the rastaman quite heard what he said but they didn't seem to care either... at least not to the point where they wanted to ask him to repeat.

"I an' I have it on tape. Can lend it to you whenever you're ready." He paused and then added reflectively, "Really thought that song was goin' to do it for me. Never sell zinc! At one point I find myself on the roads tryin' to pawn copies of it like a hitch-hikin' salesman. Jamaicans just don't appreciate cultural songs, that's all. What they want is gun-talk and—excuse my French—under-gal-frock lyrics."

"So why you don't try the U.S. market?" Hector asked mischievously. "Or England, for that matter! A song must really not be saying one damn thing for it not to sell in England. Let Sharon tell you 'bout them if you think I'm jokin; she grew up there."

"I don't have to ask the sister anythin', brother, I an' I know that people in America and England are just like they are out here on the rock. Gun-talk and under-frock—pure that. And Selassie know that if is that I must do to make it, I'm goin' to die poor."

"But I thought they said Rastas have sense! All you'd have to do is write one or two of those songs, make some good money, then you can go back to the shit you always write. If you did that, you wouldn't be in a rented back room tonight and I would be a happier man."

"Please, don't listen to Hector", Sharon said, "he's just being silly. He's awful that way."

"Easy yourself, sister, fun don't mean death to this frog, it mean fun."

"Could you just listen to that?' Hector cried. "This is the type of fart-talk we can expect to hear around here from now on."

The Rasta was silent for a while, glancing down at his instrument—the musical one, that was. "Anyway," he said at length, "I an' I goin' to get some food into the system so I'll see you guys later. And if not, tomorrow then." With this he started round the right-corner of the veranda to his door.

"By the way," Sharon called behind her, "I'm Sharon Gordon and this is my man, Hector White... What's yours?"

He paused at the opened door, one foot in, one out. "So sorry 'bout that people, it just slipped me. My passport and age paper say Joseph McCoy," he said and just before disappearing into his little den, added, "But everybody call me Cane... Sugar Cane."

CHAPTER TWO

"SUGAR CANE," Hector said and grunted. He was just getting ready for bed. Tony's seemed enticing but he wasn't going to make it tonight. The extra lessons he was offering his math class after school were really taxing on him. He'd thought of taking a break and probably resume when it was closer to their exams but decided otherwise. Maybe he could have taken the chance with the class he started with when he first moved to Brown's Hall four or so years ago but not with the groups that came after. And certainly not with this one. These boys and girls needed all the help they could get. The aptitude of the students had simply progressively worsened over the years as if the teachers at the lower level were not preparing them well enough for the rigours of final-year work. Sharon once suggested that it could also be that he wasn't teaching with the enthusiasm that he used to but he doubted this very much. Today she'd told him that some students were literally revolted by his grouchy attitude and maybe—just maybe—this contributed to their poor performance, but he doubted this very much, too. If they were any good he wouldn't have to be a grouch in the first place.

"What about him?" Sharon asked, slipping into her sky-blue nightie. Faintly, she could hear Sugar Cane moving about in his room. First impressions could sometimes be quite misleading but Sharon thought he was an okay kind of guy. *Frater could do a lot worse*, she thought. The last tenant for instance, Mr. Larry Dooms III, was drunk the night he came, vomiting all over the green tiles of the verandah and pissing in a flowerpot Sharon had on the ledge.

"Just wondering what kind of name that for a rastaman. What-ever happened to names like Bungo and Mutabaruka?"

"So because he's a rastaman he has to have those names? As far as I know, Rastafarianism is ever changing and they can have almost any name they want." She climbed into bed and reached for the Anthony Winkler novel she had waiting on the night table.

"Ever changing? You mean fuckin' confused! They don't know the next step to make. They're like chickens runnin' round with their heads cut off." He hung his clothes in the closet and started pacing the room. As if inspired, he rushed to the tele-phone. "You know somethin'? I'm goin' to give Frater a call right now and find out who the hell him think I am." Hector grabbed the receiver from the cradle and dialed the number he knew from memory. "Think we're going to just swallow every single thing he throws at us," he was saying under his breath as he waited for someone to answer. No one did. Apparently Paul Frater wasn't in. Hector kissed his teeth irritatedly and slammed the receiver back in its cradle. He got into bed and shuffled under the sheet. "Remind me–," he started but then said, "As a matter of fact you don't have to remind me for I can't forget to call him and find out what him dealin' with." Fluffing the pillow he flicked out the light on his side and rested his head.

8

Like in a TV sitcom, it was at this exact moment that the guitar started playing. The sound carried as if Sugar Cane were just by the bedside. Hector would have found such a scene in a sitcom quite amusing but this certainly wasn't. He tried putting the pillow over his ears but it wasn't working. He then threw it aside and swung his legs to the floor. Sharon's bright eyes followed him as he plodded across the room and hammered his fist against the wall. "Hey! Dready, let me tell you from now," he shouted. "This night noise shit not goin' to work with me. I have to get my sleep for unlike some of us I'm a hard workin' man and I need my rest!"

The sudden silence on the other side was broken as Sugar said, "Sorry 'bout that brother. Didn' realise I an' I was disturbin' you." He paused, then added, "It won' happen again."

"It better damn-well not!" Hector threatened as he started back for bed. He had shut the fucker up. Satisfaction beamed from his bleary eyes. As he climbed back into bed, hopefully for the last time tonight, he was feeling a little sorry that the beast didn't try to argue so he could tell him just where to go push that guitar of his and play *Jingle Bells*.

Sharon rested the novel, spread-eagled, on her bosom. "Must you always be so crude, Hector?" she asked, her eyes piercingly scrutinizing him. "No wonder your students are afraid of you."

"Yes! Call a spade a spade." He pulled the cover up way over his head and burrowed deep. His back turned to her. "And my students aren't afraid of me, they just respect authority."

They're afraid alright, Sharon thought but said nothing. One thing about being a district nurse was that you were also a psychologist. Whether you liked it or not. People of all ages told you

9

things they probably wouldn't say to anyone else. And they expected you to keep them to yourself, too.

It was just today while dressing a gash on Angela Harrison's shoulder that she realised just how much some students feared Hector. Angela's doctor had referred her to the clinic for dressing to be done to a wound she got falling from a tree. But Sharon suspected differently.

"Did Mrs. Harrison do this to you, Angela?" she asked bluntly as she went about cleansing the affected area. Claudette Fagan, the other nurse that worked at the clinic had left early for her grandfather's funeral so at just after three in the afternoon they were the only ones there. Apart from Claudette's absence, this was usually the case at this time of day.

"No nurse," Angela had answered, twitching every time the cleansing swab whisked at the gash. "Is drop a drop off of the bread fruit tree." At this time her back was turned to Sharon and she was apparently staring at a poster on the aqua-blue wall in front of her. The poster had an unfolded condom on it. The condom had legs and arms and a smiling face. *Safe sex is fun sex*, the caption read.

Sharon came around to face Angela, her charcoal-grey stockings whispering as she moved, her white uniform seeming to glow as she was not far from the afternoon daylight that came in through the window. Mitzy Harrison never spared the rod and Sharon knew this. Time after time on her way to the clinic in the mornings she would hear Mitzy hollering at one of her five daughters, "Yuh start take man now so yuh think yuh too big fi wash mi clothes! But as there is a God..." And she would trail off. You would then hear some stumbling and if you were close to the gate, actually see Mitzy administering blows to the girl with whatever her hands could clutch onto. And the child would cry, "Lawd mamma, yuh a go kill me?" And Mitzy would return, "Ki-Ki-Kill yuh yes!" Each *Ki* representing a solid blow to some part of the girl's body.

Sharon could remember going over on several occasions to ask Mitzy Harrison not to scold the girls with such ferocity.

"A fi yuh pickney?" Mitzy would shout at her. "A yuh did push them out?" The latter came out like, *a yuh did puuush dem out?*

People said that Mitzy really wasn't like this before Fred Harrison died of leukemia a few years back. Some said she had always been like this but Fred had managed to keep her in check. Some said she was crazy and called her *Mad Mitzy*. And others agreed that she was just downright horny. Nothing a good fuck couldn't cure. Whatever the real story, it was clear to Sharon that things were getting out of hand and if Angela was lying, they already *had*.

"Angie, you know you can trust me," Sharon said, staring into the girl's eyes. "I want to help you."

Angela had started sniffling at this and Sharon could see her eyes beginning to well with tears. "A know, nurse."

Sharon relaxed her tone for she could now sense she had finally begun to get somewhere. "What did–

(Mad Mitzy)

"–Mrs. Harrison use to hit you, Angie?"

11

The tear-clouds had burst now and the warm fluid bathed Angela's cheeks. She sounded as if she were choking on her tears as she said, "The maatah stick."

The mortar stick! Sharon thought, *now this is a new one.* New but not surprisingly so. People use a mortar stick to pound the hell out of coffee beans till they became powdery and Mrs. Harrison saw it the right tool to use on her child.

"Why?" Sharon then asked Angela, offering her a box of tissue.

The girl pulled some out and used it to wipe away the wetness on her face. "Because a caan' do de math Mr. White teachin'... A get dem wrong every time."

Sharon was taken aback for a while. "She did this because of that?" she asked at length, and could just picture Mitzy chasing after Angela like a club-wielding cave woman. *You start take man now so you think you too big to study you book! But as there is a God...* And of course, *Ki-Ki-Ki-Kill you yes!*

"Yes nurse," Angela sobbed. "She say a mus' always get dem right for she nuh bring nuh dunce. But nurse, me know me nuh dunce. Is just because is Mr. White teachin' why me caan' understan' for me use to understan' before him start teach me. An' me not askin' him nothin' dat me doa understan' for me nuh like how him face look when him come in de class. Me 'fraid a him."

For a little while, the fact of what Mitzy had done had left Sharon's mind as she ruminated on what Angela had said of Mr. White. *Her man!* But then, as with Mrs. Mitzy Harrison's deed, this too was new to her ears but not so surprising. And it wasn't

12

surprising either that when she argued with him about it today he couldn't accept that it was true. *My students aren't afraid of me, they just respect authority.*

Right, Sharon thought and turned a page. By this time, Hector was snoring lightly. She didn't hear Sugar Cane leave his room but now she could hear him playing his guitar somewhere outside. The melody floated through the night-air at a soft, soothing pitch. Hector grumbled something in his sleep but she didn't quite get it. *Whatever*, she thought. She rested the novel on the night table and in a while was out of bed.

Trailing the sound she went to the living room window. It gave a full view of the front-yard. With some hesitation she pulled the floral curtains away and peeked outside. And there he was: the brilliance of the full moon making him glow with a ghostly hue as he sat there on a rock under the ackee tree. A fiery red light floated in front of his lips that got brighter as he took time out to pull on it. Unless it was skin-tight, he didn't have any shirt on. Apparently, he wasn't bothered by the mountain-cool nights of Brown's Hall. He wasn't wearing a tam either and as she had figured his locks went all the way down his back. She couldn't help but admire the away he bobbed to the tune he played as his fingers marched up and down the neck of his instrument.

He stopped playing abruptly and turned to look in her direction as if he had known she was there all along. This startled her so much she could do nothing but stand there, frozen. He was peering as if he wasn't quite certain who was standing there in the window. This was good, she thought. If he was sure it was her, he would probably experience an ego boost. But it was his playing, not him, that was sparking her interest. *Really? Really.*

13

So if this is the case why did you leave your bed to come watch him play? To be closer to the music of course.

Of course.

Sugar Cane stood up, his instrument held firmly in one strong hand. The mystical silhouette looking like a dark, bronze statue. The well-defined outline suggested a name for this work of art: *The Physical Man*. With slow, certain steps the statue started toward the window.

Her first impulse was to bring her hands to her bosom, covering her exposed cleavage. Not that he could possibly see anything from where he stood but the mere thought of him looking at her like that made her a little self-conscious. And though she tried to deny it, his constant gaze made her feel a little... sexy, too. She felt as if he stared beyond the thin layer of garment and at her nakedness beneath, appreciating it. She felt that she shouldn't be liking this feeling but she did.

She loved being adored. She was still a woman, she thought. And there was a time when Hector used to stare at her in that way. But that was back in the days when he used to remember to tell her he loved her and she used to feel secure just hearing this. For after all, this was what she really wanted, someone to love her. Someone who didn't just lust for her body but genuinely wanted to spend some time with her.

Hector used to be that someone.

Sharon couldn't quite remember the exact point when Hector had started mutating to his present state but she thought she had an idea. After about a year of fruitlessly trying to conceive a baby, Sharon took the initiative to have her gynaecologist check her out. All tests showed that she was totally okay.

"He's a quack," Hector had said when she told him what she thought was pretty good news. "If you're so very okay, why aren't we seein' the results? Ask him that for ten points."

That was when she'd told him what else the doctor had to say. But before doing that she made sure he was seated in the sofa and that she was right beside him, playing with his fingers. "He's suggesting that you... go get tested, too."

"What???" he said, realising just where this was all leading. Hector got up at this and went to the kitchen for a cold beer. "Is he sayin' I may be the one at fault here?" he called back at her. It was not until he opened the fridge that he remembered he'd had the last beer the day before. With a little more force than usual he pushed the door shut and returned to the living room, pacing and running his fingers through his hair.

"He's not saying anything," Sharon had said. "He simply wants to rule out the possibility."

"–But you could tell him to rule it out, Sharon. Don't you see—first hand—how much juice I cough up every time we have sex?"

"Yes dear, but you know as well as I do that that really doesn't prove anything. Your sperm count could still be low or they could be–"

"Dead? You must be out of your mind!" He came back to sit beside her.

"Take the test, Hector; the doctor thinks you should."

"And you know what I think? I think he's a fucking moron who bought his medical degree so he could see what a pussy really looks like."

15

Nevertheless, he had gone to see a doctor with a sample of semen and ate his nails all week till the results came back. He was okay, too. Now Sharon knew. This threw a different light on things. It now meant that what they could do was try and be more strategic with their timing and positions used. At least this was what she had thought of suggesting but never quite got around to doing it, because Hector's mind was going in a totally different direction.

"Somebody's not tellin' the truth," he had grumbled to himself on that very evening just after he told her about the lab's findings.

Sharon heard the remark but couldn't quite believe that was really what she had heard. "What did you say?"

"You hear me," he said, louder now. "I said, somebody's not tellin' the truth!"

She was slow to speak. "What's that supposed to mean? Do you think I lied about the results of the HSG?"

"Bingo!"

She had slapped his face at this. "How dare you? How dare you!!" she shouted at him, her cheek muscles quivering as tears came to her eyes.

He lightly stroked the spot where she hit him. "You know I've never been a man to hide what I feel, Sharon. I can't help myself, a thing's a spade, call it a spade. That's how I am. And I strongly believe that you lied because you think that if I knew the truth I'd leave you–"

She slapped his face again, this time so hard it brought a spot of blood to the corner of his mouth. He grabbed onto her as if he was really going to crack her a good one. She trembled as she anticipated his big hand coming down on her. But it didn't happen; he stared at her watery, brown eyes for a long while and then left the house for Tony's.

They didn't talk to each other for about three days after that. Then on the fourth night, he had apologised and seduced her. The sex that night was coarse and quick as if he did it for himself only, and when he was done he rolled off her and fell asleep without a word. Maybe she was wrong, but as far as she could remember this was the first time he had treated her like this and things just never got better since.

"Hector, why are you doing this?" she had asked him one day while they had dinner.

"What am I doing?"

"You're ignoring me... You act as if I exist only as a piece of furniture in your life. You don't seem to care how I feel anymore. Why?"

He continued eating without replying. Using his tongue like a vacuum to pull in food that got stuck in his cavities.

"When you said you were sorry for calling me a liar, did you *mean* it? Or were you just so horny you'd say anything to get between my legs?"

Hector rose up and pounded the fork on the table. "Look," he said, "If I say I'm sorry, I mean I'm sorry. Now could you just get the fuck off that? *Uh?*" And again he had walked out on her sitting there.

The entire ordeal had bothered her so much that she'd even thought of going back to England to stay with her parents for a while. But then she decided against it, as she didn't think she was up to her father's whining. "I can't fathom one good reason why you would want to go to *that place*," Dr. Ronald J. Gordon had said when she told him she wanted to come to Jamaica eight years ago. "Next thing you know, you go there and start associating yourself with that ... *budubudu* music and people who take pride in knowing they are *ragamuffins!*" But then, when she told him she actually wanted to study medicine at the University of the West Indies, he relented somewhat, saying, "Well I guess that's not too bad a reason. After all the University of the West Indies, I must say is... quite good. Certainly not Oxford or Cambridge or London but, it will do."

The truth was, however, that she didn't want to study medicine. What she really wanted to do was go to nursing school. Back in England, Ronald would never have allowed it for he wanted her to study medicine and become a brilliant surgeon, "Like me." But the distance of four thousand-odd miles was considered a safe zone. And yes, she also wanted to associate with some of these people who took pride in knowing they were ragamuffins. With her mother's help she had managed to keep it secret from Ronald till she was all the way in Kingston. "Let the girl find her roots, Ron. Your parents are from Jamaica and you've never been there once!" Margaret Gordon had told Ronald while he was on the phone listening unbelievingly to Sharon's confession. *"Roots!"* Ronald had called back at her. "Who does she think she is? Alex Haley? Listen to me Sharon, don't let me walk on the sea to come and get you."

"Daddy, I'm twenty years old; I know what I want."

"You don't know what you want–," Ronald started.

"Well, even if she doesn't give her a chance to find out," Margaret had interrupted.

"Yes, Daddy, I do," Sharon had told him. And tonight as she stood here, she still thought she knew what she wanted. It was just that Hector was hardly representing it anymore.

The statue came closer still. Sharon gathered enough will-power to pull the curtains back over the window and turn away. *Don't I know what I want*, she thought, *don't I know it!*

Sharon went back to bed but couldn't sleep. And she just had to admit it to herself now, that there was something about the man outside—other than the music—that was making her feel warm and tingly all over. *Is it the locks?* She wondered. Was it the locks that had aroused her so much that she was now squeezing her groin against Hector, trying to oust the sensation from her body? Or that rugged, unshaven look?

She didn't think so. And if that had anything to do with it, it wasn't the main cause. Sharon knew that the drought had a lot to do with it too. How long had it been since she'd–

(I know what I want.)

–had sex? Four, five weeks? A month and a half? She'd actually lost count. And the times she had done it before the drought began weren't worth mentioning anyway for they were just as dry and one-sided as they had been for the past two years now. That's why she was feeling like this: she was *starved*. Hector wasn't interested anymore and that was just too bad for she was still so very interested.

"Hector!" Sharon whispered desperately at the man that was wrapped up like a corpse beside her. She pulled the sheet from his head and sent her tongue licking frantically at his ear. "Hector, baby wake up."

"Wha?... What is it Sharon?" he asked groggily, pulling the sheet back over his head.

"I want you, Hector... I want you to give it to me." She reached over and caressed the soft lump in his underpants. "Wake up!"

"–Tired," he grumbled. "Go to sleep." In no time he was snoring again. Sharon began patting him on the back but he didn't stir.

The guitar's melody started floating through the air again as if Sugar Cane had gone back sitting in the same place. It continued till about two in the morning. Sharon knew this for even after masturbating she just couldn't fall asleep.

CHAPTER THREE

"YOU WANT it? Alright! Here, take it!" Hector climbed ferociously on top of the sleeping woman. Reeling her panties down and spreading her legs with such urgency it literally jolted her awake. "Take it!" This came out, *tek it!*, as he slammed his hardness into her, his breath hot and sour in her face. Involuntarily her arms clutched him round the back as he plummeted into her. She wasn't as frightened as one would expect though for this had happened before. Hector didn't want much these days, but when Hector wanted Hector took, no questions asked.

"Take it..." He stroked her again only now with considerably less power. "Wind, goddammit," he told her. "You're actin' like you not loving' it. Wind your ass!"

"Hec–," she began but his big, sour tongue was in her mouth too soon, the stubble of his chin grating her cheeks. Obeying his request Sharon Gordon rotated her hips once, twice, th–

"Jeeesuss!!!" Hector went from behind clenched teeth, eyelids fluttering uncontrollably. "I'm comin'... *Jeeesusss!"*

21

It wasn't long after this that he fell off her and hauled himself to the bathroom. Sharon laid there silently, her nightie crumpled up just above her navel and her panty wrapped around one ankle. Why was she allowing this to happen? It wasn't like she didn't know it was all wrong and she certainly wasn't liking it—so why not just leave? She had enough money to get some other place to rent on her own for she had always kept her bank account in a tidy order. "Always keep your own savings account," she could remember her mother warning her while she was getting ready to leave home. "And never let your man have equal control over your money unless you're married to him. Even then you should still have something somewhere that you can pull on if things get fuzzy." Sharon had never forgotten these words and now she couldn't help but saying, thank God for that. For at least now, if she finally decided to leave, money wouldn't be a factor to keep her back. *And if push comes to shove I could always get a job at a hospital and live in the nurses' cottages.*

So a place to stay wasn't her excuse for remaining in this predicament. It was more like the Crazy Glue syndrome that so many people had to deal with. You had all right to leave, you couldn't see a reason to stay yet you remained. Why? *Maybe because I'm dumb*, she thought. *Or maybe it's because, like most people, I think that things are going to get back to the way they used to be.*

While she tried to figure herself out, she could hear the toilet bowl gargling Hector's piss. The clock on the dresser alarmed six a.m.

"Fuck you," Hector said as he farted. He flushed the toilet and was quick to realise that the tank was not refilling itself. This meant one of two things: either the water was gone or the pressure was so low it couldn't make it to the house. The first would mean a disaster for he hadn't a drop in storage. The second, however, wasn't so bad as there was a stand pipe in the back yard that usually had water even in low pressure situations. All he'd have to do then was fill up a wash pan for his bath and a bucket or two in case full pressure was not restored for a while. Living in Brown's Hall you got used to this way of thinking, for you either experienced low pressure or no water at all at least once every two weeks. That was why most people kept steel drums or massive water tanks at home.

"A goin' get a water tank installed tomorrow so you guys doa have to worry too much about the water problems we have up here," Paul Frater had told them when they had first moved here from Kingston to discover that the bathroom and kitchen had absolutely no water and appeared to have been dry for a little while. "In the mean time you can just use up the stand pipe to catch water for bathin' and the likes." And after a pause he had added, "Those who doa like bathin' in a wash pan can always use the river. It not far from here—'bout a mile and a half."

A mile and a half, not far? Hector had thought then and said, "What do you think, baby?" For this had been a time when her opinion mattered.

Sharon had looked around at the big picture then. "The house is nice," she said, "and it's cheap." After all this was what they were really looking for, so they could save a little to buy their own in the near future. Kingston never offered such a combination. It was either safe, comfortable, stylish and expensive or slummy and cheap. Before deciding to even consider a place as

23

rural as Brown's Hall, Hector had suggested to Sharon that if she didn't think she was up to the far away location she could probably have her parents give them a loan to buy a house and they could both work and repay it over time—but she had said no. "I think I want to know what it's like walking without my *parents* as crutches," she told him.

"Okay then," Hector said to Frater, "We'll take it."

"Good thinkin'," Frater said and handed them the keys. "I don' know if this mean anythin' to you but some very important people use to stay here–"

"It doesn't, really," Hector said.

"Well, to each his own, Mama always use to say." As he walked away to his Land Rover by the gate he said, "have fun guys, and remember the rent is due month end. The tank will be in by tomorrow."

That was four years ago and the tank was still not here. Hector used to call and ask him about it but after hearing, "Tomorrow," and, "Next week-end," for about two years he simply decided to let it be. It wasn't like he was planning on spending the rest of his life here anyway.

Hector pulled on his pants, went to the kitchen and opened the hard wood door that faced the back yard. It was his intention to check the stand pipe for water, and if it had any, fill up the bucket and then fetch some for his bath. But the shock of what he was faced with when the door came open was so overwhelming that for a while he just stood there not believing the sight of it.

"What a *rass* man slack!" Hector exclaimed.

Sharon got up as she wondered what on earth could he be

talking about now. She pulled her drawers on and quickly stumbled to the bedroom window which opened to the back yard. Sugar Cane was perched on a rock by the stand pipe. He was taking a bath. *Oh my God*, she thought. The man was soaking his washrag under the tap and using it to scrub his body like he wanted to wash the colour from his skin. But it wasn't the way he washed himself that intrigued Sharon to the point that her heart raced uncontrollably in her chest. It was the sight of his instrument that was causing it, the God-given one that swung pendulously between his firm, coffee-brown legs. Her mouth fell open in awe when her brain registered the fact that the two instruments she had come to know thus far—Hector's and that of her two-month-long boyfriend before him—looked like thimbles when compared to the young elephant's trunk this brother was sporting.

"Dready, you don't have a bathroom?" Hector hollered.

Sugar Cane glanced up through dripping wet locks which had fallen into his face. He was only just realising that he was being watched. "I an' I bathroom pipe dry, brethren," he said. "Look like the pressure too low to reach the house."

"But wha' the fuck...? You can't put a wash pan in it like everybody else?" Hector asked.

Sugar Cane shook his head understandably. "But I an' I is not like everybody else, brother," he said, "I an' I is Rasta. Rasta nuh bath in a wash pan. The landlord tell me about a river near here. I an' I would go down there but guess what? Wake up late!" He paused to reach for a towel he'd hung on the nearby clothes line. While proceeding to dry himself he added, "But anyway, we is all adults; what I an' I have on I body is nothing' strange to any of us. We've all seen it before."

But never this generous, Sharon thought, a bubble of laughter just stopping at the brink of her throat. She swallowed it promptly.

"Listen man," Hector said, "this is not a display shop nor no damn Garden of Eden. And above all principle is principle. Suppose someone pass by the fence or come by to see me? What you think they'd say when them see you with this big rass *hood* for public viewin'? That I'm hostin' a freak show here, that's what they'd think!"

"Alright brother," Sugar Cane said as he wrapped the towel about him and started for his room. "It won't happen again."

"Pshaw!" Hector went as he kissed his teeth and went back to the bedroom. Sharon was only just leaving the window, still trying hard not to just burst out in a fit of laughter. *I an'I is Rasta? Is so it goin' to go?* With this thought in mind he sat by the bedside, took the telephone to his lap and started dialing Frater's number. He said to Sharon, "You see for yourself now why I don't think it's a good idea to have that type of *beast* livin' in the same yard with us? Suppose we had children? You know what psychological damage such a picture could cause them?"

Sharon remained silent to all this as she got herself ready to go to the kitchen to make breakfast. Sometimes, she thought, it was best to just let him talk till he felt like stopping.

After several rings the sleepy voice of Paul Frater answered the phone. *"What?"* it said.

"Mornin' Mr. Frater," Hector began. His pitch had fallen to that of a reasonable man. "Is what type of animal you've put to live with us, sir?"

26

There was silence for a little while as if Frater was thinking. Either that or he had dozed off again. "You mean the dreadlocks?" he said finally.

"Who the fuck else you think I'm talkin'?" Hector shouted back at the phone.

"Alright Hector, calm yuh'self. What him do now?"

"What him do? The man bathin' stark naked in the back yard and when I talk to him, him tellin' me *that I an' I is Rasta an'* all sort o' fart!"

Silence.

"You serious?" Paul Frater asked. "Alright a goin' talk to him tomorr–"

"Don't tell me shit 'bout tomorrow, man, that's always your line. Come and see about this man now. *Right now!"*

"Alright. A will be down there in a little bit... just give me a chance to put on some clothes and get some coffee."

Paul Frater did drop by that morning as he had said he would but by the time he got there Sugar Cane had already left the house.

CHAPTER FOUR

SUGAR CANE bundled out of the Nissan cab as soon as it got into Spanish Town. He was hardly able to feel his own legs. Eleven persons had been stuffed in the cab this time and according to the driver, if the car didn't need servicing he probably would have made space for at least two more of those left behind. "Hurt me to have to leave the people them behind when a know them want to reach town early for work, but wha' to do?" Samuel Sheggs had said as he was pulling out of Brown's Hall Crossroads, leaving a dozen or more of the district's working class eagerly awaiting a ride. *So what 'bout the money Mr. Sheggs? Sugar Cane thought. You sure that's not the real reason you want to take as much of these people as you can? Do you really care anythin' 'bout them gettin' to work early? Or are you just takin' advantage of their need to get to work early?*

This was actually his third experience and Sugar Cane still couldn't figure out exactly how it was done. And he knew that if he should tell anyone who had never actually seen it they'd first think the weed he was smoking had finally gone to his head. *For really, he thought, how can eleven people hold in a car? And to think, I an' I is actually a part of it and I still can't believe it.* Sugar Cane had expressed his amazement to the passenger whose ass was lodged just between Sugar Cane's rib cage and his hip bone. He hoped she wouldn't fart for that would just be too bad. "The record is twenty-two," the woman had returned. *Guess I an' I should be thankin' Selassie for his small mercies then,* he thought.

He paid Mr. Sheggs, got his guitar from the trunk and started across Cumberland Road, stomping his legs as he went, trying to get the blood circulating properly. When he breathed he felt a slight pain in his side where the woman had to rest her ass. He was still thankful that she hadn't farted, however. The minor pain would go away with each breath but as to whether he could have survived a fart at such close range was a matter for the jury to decide. Sugar Cane smiled.

By the time his legs got fully functional he had reached where he was going. He put his guitar directly ahead of him to navigate properly up the narrow flight of steps that led to the Jamtouch Recording Studio. This was where he had to rush off to yesterday morning, just after moving in. Trying to get an audition, he had arrived at about six but was still too late. Quite a number of hopefuls had come in before. And after sitting in the waiting area for an entire day he was informed that they wouldn't be seeing anybody else till the first Monday in January. Now this was a whole three months away and he certainly didn't wish to wait that long. Who would? The thought of just how your life can change after an audition was simply too overwhelming for anyone with the dream of selling a song to want to wait that long. Now Sugar

Cane considered himself a proud man but he was also a realist, so he begged them to see him sooner. And after about ten solid minutes of nothing but this they relented and told him to come in this morning at seven forty-five.

There was someone already in the waiting area when he finally got there. *Must do some real ass kissin' like I an' I to get here,* he thought.

"Greetin's brother," Sugar Cane smiled as he found a seat on the opposite side of the lobby. The man nodded in return. There were several magazines on a wicker shelf next to him. Sugar Cane selected one with Burning Spear on the cover and started flipping through.

"Wha' the time, boss?" the man across the floor asked.

Sugar Cane glanced at his wrist watch. "Seven ten." And for the first time he thought that Sam Sheggs' timing hadn't been too bad after all. Forty minutes to cover fifteen miles in a BMW Z3 roadster and on a freeway would have been atrocious but when done in a ten-year-old car that shimmied on a pothole-mottled, corkscrew road it was damn good going. *Damn dangerous, too,* he thought, but he was glad he was early.

"Mr. Touch say him would come by six but a caan' see him yet," the other said. He was slim built and no more than twenty with low-cut, curly hair. He was rather expensively dressed yet he didn't seem the type who could afford the clothes he wore—but this was quite the usual thing for young entertainers who had just started making a little money. Soon, Sugar Cane thought, he would get a facial and manicured nails and a good dentist and everything would fall into place. A ratchet spun from its ring on the youth's index finger.

"They'll soon come now," Sugar Cane assured him.

And it wasn't two minutes after he spoke that the noise started at the foot of the stairs. Four well fed and well-dressed men bustled their way up, retelling all of last night's jokes with echoing laughs that literally vibrated the walls of the lobby. One of the men was constantly kept in the lead. He owned the place. The other guys were his technical assistants or—more appropriately put—his sidekicks. They laughed at all his jokes and agreed with every-thing he said.

"Wait!" Harold Touch exclaimed as he got to the top of the stairs. "Sugar Cane, you here again?" He chuckled and the men beside him laughed like they'd never heard a funnier joked. Ap-parently this was what they got paid for.

"Well, you know how it is, brother Touch," Sugar Cane an-swered. "Can't really stop tryin' till the breath leave the body."

"I hope you have somethin' marketable this time round or that might not be far from now," Touch commented and giggled. The three sidekicks laughed haughtily as they followed him be-hind French doors that separated the offices from the lobby.

"Sound like you come here a lot, dreadlocks," the man across the room said.

Sugar Cane sighed. "Been comin' here for ages, brother... As far back as I an' I can remember." And he wasn't exaggerating either. He used to come here as a child, dashing over after school to gawk at entertainers with much awe as they came and went about their business. The Rastafarian ones had impressed him most and he would dream of some day being an entertainer too. Back then though, the studio was called Garlander, and John

31

Garland was a more amicable producer to deal with than Touch. At least more amicable to Rastafarians. He wasn't a Rastafarian himself but he had an interest in cultural songs. Sugar Cane's only single to date had been produced by John. As a matter of fact, it was John Garland's last production before he was robbed and murdered at his St. Jago Heights home back in '88. To this date some people still held that Touch had something to do with John's death. They really didn't have a reason, but felt that Touch was the kind of person who would do that sort of thing to get ahead. And the hunch was cemented a year later when Touch bought the studio and changed the name. *Maybe bought it with the same money he took from John,* Sugar Cane had thought.

Touch's rise to the throne was a major setback for not just Sugar Cane but every Rastafarian musician in Spanish Town. It was like the *Grand Ole Opry* getting new management who didn't particularly like country music. And it didn't seem as if it was a case where he didn't like Rastafarian songs. It was more like those songs weren't making the sort of money he was interested in. This had forced Sugar Cane to travel the country in search of a producer only to discover that most of them were either of the same heart as Touch or worse.

"Them afraid of promotin' the truth, brethren," Sugar Cane's long time friend David 'Jah-Jah Son' Campbell had told him one day as they both walked home from an entire day of rejections. They had been friends since St. Jago High School where they both did A'levels but decided to follow careers in music, instead of the more sure path of going on to university. Jah-Jah Son's ultimate goal, though, was not to write songs but produce them. Singing and song writing were just stepping stones he would always think. "They don't want to be set free," Jah-Jah Son had concluded.

"Well, I hope them change them mind soon for, Selassie know, I an' I growin' weary," Sugar Cane had said.

"You?" Jah-Jah Son said; "I an' I don't think so, Cane. I don't think so at all."

"Why not? If things not workin' out you don't think one day I an' I goin' stop tryin'?"

"Not when you love that somethin' as much as I know the I love writin' songs. You always goin' to be givin' it that one last try. An' you always goin' to tell you'self that if it don't work out this time, that's it. But that won't be it for this is who you are. If you stop writin' songs you'll be so tormented you'll start writin' them again. Jah know!"

"I don't have to keep writin' songs an' pretty soon I guess I an' I will give it up. But one dream I'll always be doin' time with, is producin' good songs like you'll be writin' in a few years."

"So you don't think I songs good now?"

Jah-Jah Son had looked matter-of-factly at him at this. "No," he had said. "But we both young an' we have a long way to go. We have hope."

Since then Jah-Jah Son had given up song writing; got married and started a roadside soup kitchen which steadily grew into a small restaurant at 56 Burke Road. Business wasn't the best but he hoped that some day it would assist him in getting where he wanted to go. And if that didn't work he would try something else. For after all, that was what it was all about, hope.

"So the I is a deejay?" Sugar Cane asked the man across the room.

"Yeah man," the man said.

Somehow Sugar Cane could always be able to just guess the deejays and singers. He wasn't sure how he did it though. Maybe it was just that the deejays mostly spoke hoarsely and were often rather pensive. On the other hand, he had found singers to be mostly jovial and erratic, always singing a part of their favorite song so you could hear the wonderful voice they had. At least this was how he observed the newcomers to be. With the seasoned ones it was harder to tell for they all behaved alike.

"Ever hear 'bout Point-4-5?" the youth asked proudly.

Sugar Cane nodded several times. He had been seeing the name on a few small-time dance hall posters all over the place. In a few weeks he should be performing at a dance at the Brown's Hall Primary School, too. "You?"

"Yeah man!" Point-4-5 smiled.

Out of curiosity, Sugar Cane asked, "How long you been in the business?"

"Long, long time, man. My first stage name was Culture King! An' for a long time—'bout five years—that was the name but it never work! So about a year ago I decide to try out this new image an' I start seein' progress instantly. Fi real, dreadlocks, if you even want to do culture later on it best to get two or so rude boy tune on the road so you can survive till people start listenin' the conscious lyrics you have to give."

Just last night, Sugar Cane remembered, Hector was saying the very same thing ... only in a sarcastic way.

Without notice Point-4-5 decided to give a sample of his lyrics: *"'Cause me talk 'bout the 'matic an' mi talk 'bout the gloc... sometime mi go dung unda gal frack: Christian si mi an' a talk seh mi slack. True dem nuh know a di system want dat. System want dat, system get dat. You ha' fi do di backa lash jus' fi mek some cash..."* He broke off laughing. "Fi real, dreadlocks," he then said after clearing his throat, "is how you have to run things if you want to get the money before you whistle blow."

Fi real.

Sugar Cane smiled but said nothing.

One of the sidekicks came out. He was a heavily bearded man whose eyes shifted constantly as if he always expected someone to catch him red-handed. He beckoned Point-4-5 who got up and disappeared behind the French doors with him.

One hour passed. By this six other young entertainers—all men—came crowding the lobby and another four or five technical staffers of the studio went inside, their ID cards clipped to their shirts like federal agents. A well-dressed, expensive-cologne-wearing man passed into the studio also. Must be another deejay, Sugar Cane thought for everybody hailed him as he sweet-stepped his way out of sight.

In another half hour the same sidekick stuck his big head out, found Sugar Cane and used an index finger to invite him inside. And time enough, Sugar Cane thought for he was getting quite weary of just sitting there. The burly man led him through an inner lobby, with which he was quite familiar, to the door of Touch's office. He opened the door and saw him in.

"Have a seat, Sugar Cane," Touch said from behind the posh

mahogany desk. Directly behind him was a glass case with quite a number of record trophies and awards. Apparently he was doing something right. *Either that or the music industry was terribly wrong.*

Sugar Cane found a seat in one of the two brown leather chairs in front of the desk. Touch was more than ten years his senior but looked just as young since he could afford himself such luxuries as facials and face lifts. His clothes were splendid and he reeked of Polo Sport. *But you still look like a rat,* Sugar Cane thought.

"Culture?" Touch asked with an air of impatience as he used the remote to switch off the Kenwood stereo system at the far corner of the office. The air conditioning here was cold compared to that of the lobby.

"Definitely," said Sugar Cane with conviction.

Here we go again, Harold Touch's eyes seemed to say. He sighed. "Is it any good?"

"Culture is always good, brother."

"You know what I mean, Sugar Cane, so don't play games. Does it sound like somethin' marketable?"

"Guess you'll be the judge of that," Sugar Cane said.

Touch sighed again. "Alright. Let's hear it."

Sugar Cane took out his guitar from its canvas case. After taking a moment to find the correct notes he began a low, nervous singing which picked up to full stride as he went along.

NEVER SAY DIE

by Sugar Cane

VERSE 1:

There are people in this world

who have champagne with dinner.

People in this world

who a natural born winner.

But the opposite is also true.

Yes there are people like me an' you,

Like me an' you, so true so true.

CHORUS:

But we ain't gonna say die,

an' we'll never stop, no,

For the day is gonna come

when we'll be winners too.

An' the light of Rastafari

will carry us through;

All we got to do

is believe.

(Repeat chorus once.)

VERSE 2:

Some have fought the struggle

till they tired an' old.

From they born till they die

they walking' in the cold;

But with faith we must pull through.

For with positive thoughts

We can wither the storm, an' we carry on!

BRIDGE:

'Cause we ain't gonna say die an' we'll never stop, no.

Fail a evenin' but a mornin' we still on the go.

An' the light of Jah Selassie, I will carry us through,

All we got to do is believe.

(Repeat bridge twice and fade)

He sang his heart out, sending the notes to hit against the roof of his mouth. They resounded in the typical reggae timber style he had developed over the years. And when he was done he rested the guitar back on his lap as he awaited the verdict. This was always a nerve-rattling experience for him. It was like having a child and waiting for the doctors to say whether it was healthy or not.

Touch rubbed his palms as if for warmth, as he thought. "It sounds... okay," he said finally, "But it's too long..."

Sugar Cane wasn't quite understanding. "Too long?" he asked.

"Yes, it's taking too long to get to the chorus. And the chorus isn't swinging as it should for it to grab music-buyers' attention. People catch onto short, snappy choruses like, *Telephone love, sounds so sweet on my mind. Telephone love, make my day every time.* An' it's done. People not looking for this long, deep thing like it's some Psalms you're writing. And especially so when you're not saying exactly what they want to hear. Tell us about man-woman romance, hard core sex machine, how you're wicked in bed or how many men one bullet from your gun can slaughter. It's strange, I know, but this is what people buy. The *Jah seh this, Jah seh that* won't work. It might work for a few people like Everton Blender and Luciano but I'm not here to put my money on the exceptions. I want the motherfuckin' *rule.*"

Sugar Cane sighed. "So you keep tellin' I."

"And so you keep not listening! Cane, this thing is not about religion nor right or wrong; it's about money. Dollars! And until you're prepared to give me lyrics that can make me make back my money and a little extra I can't help you."

Sugar Cane got up with the pride of Paul Bogle. "Like I said, I an' I won't stop tryin'. One day, one day one of you producers must give me a chance." He returned the guitar to its case as he got ready to leave.

Touch chuckled and used the remote to turn the stereo back on. "You're a creative man, Cane, so you really shouldn't stop trying," he said. "But while you're at it, fuck some pussy. I hear it helps in the creative process." Touch started giggling as if he were being tickled by the devil. "And as you well know, if you have a problem getting some, feel free to let me know so I can invite you to my next pool side get-together. Girls will be there to

39

eat your shit if you want them to." He winked. "Think about it."

"Thanks for your time, Mr. Touch," Sugar Cane said and left the office.

And even as he came down the staircase to the now-crowded streets of Spanish Town, he was still hearing Touch's bubbly giggles in his head.

CHAPTER FIVE

IT WAS a Leyland bus named Treasure Hunter that he boarded back to Brown's Hall. The huge machine was painted with vertical stripes of rainbow colours, just like the tam he had on, the name written on the side and back in Old English lettering. Everyone was seated but the bus still seemed somewhat cramped as the entire stretch of passageway was mounding with boxes and baskets and live chickens with their legs tied so they couldn't move far. Of course, all this and the smell of gas oil and perspiration in the humid air could prove taxing on the nostrils if you weren't a regular. Sugar Cane was lucky he got a window seat so he could stick his head out every now and then to take in fresh air without letting it seem obvious. Nobody else appeared to be having a problem however, and they all seemed to know each other by name. It's like a little market place, he thought. But this was not surprising for most of these people actually vended at the Spanish Town market.

Several conversations happened throughout the length of the bus, like a classroom with the teacher absent. It was hard to figure out what people were talking about because of this, but every now and then Sugar Cane might pick up a line such as, *"Yes, missis, every day dat God send di man tek soap wash di piss pot an' use it cook–"*. He would probably lose them at this and after a while catch on to, *"But Frank mad? A mus' mad him mad! Tell Jackie fi carry him go dacta before it get too bad."* And somebody else saying, *"It bad a'ready. Anybody weh righted can cook in a piss pot?"* Sugar Cane couldn't help feeling like an intruder listening in on all this but nevertheless had to agree that *Frank mus' mad.*

Sugar Cane had gone to see Jah-Jah Son today just after his visit with Touch. It was the only way he could think of to get rid of some of the rage that built up in him after the producer had flatly refused a song Sugar Cane thought was going to be the one. Yes, he had thought *Prestigious Dogs* would have been *the one,* too, but at least it got a chance to prove that it wasn't. *Never Say Die* was a real pet of his, and seeing that he considered himself more mature now than he had been when he wrote *Dogs,* he believed that it should have been given a chance too. He believed it to be his best effort since *Dogs* and that the moment Touch heard the first verse and chorus he would simply tell him to stop and instantly commence to make up a contract. But it wasn't to be. Once again the man with the money had turned him away without a second thought. *Not even a second thought!*

"I don' know what we do them, Sugar Cane," Jah-Jah Son had said after Sugar Cane told him of what was disturbing him. They were both seated on wooden stools at the back of the restaurant enjoying the ital stew Jah-Jah Son had provided, on the house. He had extracted about two teeth from the top row recently, so when he spoke he had a slight lisp. "They just don' think we should get a chance. Jah know!" He paused as he ate and then added. "All a song like this would be the right thing for I an' I to produce but I don' know when my plans goin' to work out. Took a small loan from the bank to develop this place a little bit. If all go well, I an' I plan to make it more attractive so the big shot them who drive by on the highway will want to stop an' spend some money with I an' I."

"Well," Sugar Cane had said scooping up what was left in the bowl, "the food taste good so once they stop they will always be comin' back for more."

"Is that I want," Jah-Jah Son replied. "For that would mean I an' I could pay off the loan an' start concentratin' the profit on *the dream*. Irie?"

"Irie," Sugar Cane had answered in full understanding.

"All in all though you know, brethren," Jah-Jah Son continued, "you're still not the worse for at least the I's been able to live off it alone till now. Some people so bad—or get treated so bad— that they have to give it up an' go plant corn or sell broom. Not that plantin' corn an' sellin' broom is a bad thing but, when it not what you want to do, it can feel like a prison sentence."

Sugar Cane had looked into this quite seriously and had to agree with his friend. His songs weren't being bought but at least he still got odd jobs every now and then at cheap-paying north coast clubs to perform. At least he still had a foot in the business. This was a better deal than many people had. And Jah-Jah Son himself had told him some years ago while they walked home from that day of dismal auditions, he had hope. He was a little older now, yes, but he still had hope.

43

Still!

It was this visit to his friend and the positive outlook it re-stored in him that gave Sugar Cane renewed vitality. He wasn't the man to mope about when defeated, but the rejection had re-ally hit him hard. Now it was in the past and all he had to do was move on. At least for now, this was how Sugar Cane felt.

As he tried to relax, he rested his head against the back of the seat and gazed out the window. The wind was gentle on his face as the overweight bus farted its way up the mountain road. He gradually became aware of just how wonderful these country bus rides could be. He actually felt like a tourist... well, a tourist in a smelly country bus was probably more like it. The green, ram-bling hills were actually as beautiful as they were on the profes-sionally photographed postcards. Only now you could also smell fresh, lung-cleansing air. And because of the added height of the bus as opposed to Samuel Sheggs' ten-year-old Nissan Sunny, the precipice that skirted the road seemed to really deserve all the respect the driver was giving it.

Despite the glory of it all, however, sleep was almost inevi-table on a slow, long, winding ride such as this. Sugar Cane slept intermittently. He would wake up only to see more green hills and just go blank again as the engines droned monotonously in his head. Apparently this ride was going to take twice the time Samuel Sheggs' had taken this morning. *Lucky I don't have an appointment,* he thought in the haze as he drifted off again.

When he did come awake for any length of time it was the sister back at the house that was popping up in his mind. *Sister*

Sharon Gordon, he thought, *what a sweet woman*. When he had first seen her sitting there last night he was going to complement her on her rather pleasant disposition but her man didn't seem the type with whom he could take such a risk. From what he had experienced of Hector White thus far, he knew he was a very miserable man who searched for things to bother himself with. As far as he could tell—which really wasn't very far—Hector cramped Sharon's free-spirited, easygoing style. And he wondered how did a woman so pure get hooked up with a man like Hector. Then again maybe she was no different from Hector; Sugar Cane probably just hadn't seen that part of her yet.

No, he told himself, that sister is definitely sweet from the core out. He could see nothing false in the way she had presented herself last night. And it was probably just sheer bad luck that brought her and Hector together. Sugar Cane remembered Hector mentioning she had grown up in England, so he also wondered why was she working as a district nurse in Jamaica. Bell boys in England got more money than nurses in Jamaica—so what was the story? It certainly couldn't be Hector for he wasn't worth a sacrifice of such magnitude. It would more be a case where she—for some reason or the other—had to come to Jamaica, got into severe difficulty, and had no choice but to shack up with Hector to save her skin. This was what Sugar Cane thought.

Last night when he had turned and seen the curvy silhouette in the window seemingly appreciating his music, it had made him feel good inside, for he'd thought, *she likes I music*. But when he'd got up to thank her for making his night and ask if there was anything she would like to hear, she had turned away.

Now he wasn't quite sure what to make of this. He hoped she wasn't thinking he resented her standing there looking at him, for that would have been so far from the truth.

After a series of hemming and hawing, the bus finally pulled its ass to a halt at the Brown's Hall Crossroads. By this all the talking and laughing had simmered to a distinct stare of fatigue. And to think this was by no means the final stop made Sugar Cane actually feel pity for the people who would be getting off after another six miles at places like Ginger Ridge.

First off the bus, he wobbled across the road and went straight to his room where he threw himself across the bed. The beautiful experience of the bus ride was very draining but then he thought, *isn't that usually the case with beautiful experiences?* He slept for an hour and a half.

It was about five-thirty when he woke up. He could smell food. *The sister must be makin' dinner for her man,* he thought. Sugar Cane took off his tam and lay there for a little bit, getting his thoughts together before eventually getting up. He took the guitar and went outside to sit under the ackee tree just like he had last night. In no time he started searching the strings for a tune.

As if the guitar had the power of the Pied Piper's pipe, on hearing the tune Sharon floated out to the veranda. She was dressed for the kitchen in a full plaid apron and head scarf. There was a big cook-spoon in her hand. When he saw her he didn't stop playing like he had last night, however. Instead he tried to better himself, making the strings sound louder and clearer without missing a single note. It was just like he would have played if he were on a stage on the north coast. And just as he was hoping, Sharon started toward where he sat. Her eyes, a very dark brown, were so beautiful, he was thinking as she came up to him. To his surprise she didn't just stand there but actually sat down on a rock beside him, looking attentively at his hands as they found the right strings to pluck. Now this caused him to stop playing as his concentration, for some strange reason, simply went. He smiled at her and shook his head in disbelief. No one had ever done this to him before.

"Did I cause that?" Sharon asked pulling away uncertainly, concerned.

"No sister," he promptly lied. "I was just not thinkin' straight, that's all."

"I really didn't mean to disturb you... If you prefer I could lea–"

"Stay!" he told her quickly, just short of holding her hand and pulling her back. "Not disturbin' I an' I at all, sister. Like I said it was just a little stray thinkin' that cause it. No fault of yours at all. And besides, I was just startin' anyway; not much you could disturb me from." This said, he hurriedly started a tune. "See what I mean?"

Sharon nodded, smiling. She had only just turned off the stove with the intention to go have a bath when she heard the guitar. *He's here*, she'd thought and then asked herself, *so what?* The answer came quickly, *you can go and listen to him play, that's so what.* This she thought was enough justification for the anxiety that had welled inside her when she heard the music. She simply wanted to hear him play.

47

However she had felt last night and whatever she had thought was causing it, was a matter of circumstance. She was vulnerable and he had represented what she wanted. That was all. Any fool sitting there last night playing a guitar or just plain sitting there would quite likely have made her feel the very same way. Matter of circumstances. She was only happy that she had not thought of going out there last night. For though nothing would have happened, he probably would have sensed her predicament and thought she was some kind of slut. Or that she was the kind of girl who cheated on her man every chance she got. But Sharon Marva Gordon was neither of these. As a matter of fact, sometimes she thought she was too accommodating to Hector's expectations of what a woman *should* be. Rushing home from work every day to make dinner while he lounged about in the staff room playing dominoes after he was done with extra lessons. Then he'd come home and she'd serve dinner while he watched TV and if he wasn't too tired after dinner he'd slide over to Tony's where he would remain till it was time for bed. Maybe if she had been at least giving him reason to believe there might be a chance of her fooling around he'd pay more attention to his homework. And homework didn't just mean sex, it also meant being around for healthy conversations which didn't always lead to an argument. It also meant caring enough to ask how her day was at the clinic, was it crowded, like today had been? Or was it just the usual slow drawl of five or so patients for the entire day? This probably didn't mean much to some women but to Sharon Gordon it meant being alive. And especially so because she really didn't have a whole lot of friends who she could probably call up and pass the time.

48

She really didn't have any friends in Browns Hall. At least not any that she would feel like spending hours chatting with. There were several acquaintances, yes, but this was as far as it went for the most part. It wasn't that she was antisocial in any way either, it was more that she chose very carefully the people she called friends. And if social standing was ever a factor in her selection process, it was in favour of people who weren't regarded as having any. Socialites who believed they should know you or want to talk to you because of who you were, made her stomach turn. Her closest girlfriends, for instance, were Ruby Smith and Grace Hogan who were vendors at the Spanish Town market. Only they didn't live in Brown's Hall but eight miles further up the mountain at a place called Simon. And telephone lines had not reached that far up as yet. Sharon had met the *Terrible Two-some* (Sharon had coined the name because of the ludicrous conversations they were always initiating) on her first ever visit to the market. She had been looking for a good buy on yellow yam when she happened upon them. Normally she would have bought it from the yam farmers in Brown's Hall but at the time Brown's Hall was experiencing a slump in its yam production.

"If you buy this an' you don' think is the bes' yellow yam you ever taste," Ruby had said to her from behind the stall, "Carry back what lef' an' I'll give you back you money an' another pound. Is pum-pum yam this type of yellow yam name. It's the bes' any-where, try it." She had tried it and was so impressed that it was all she asked for whenever she went to the market these days. And even though Brown's Hall's crop had improved since, she still went to the market to buy from Ruby and Grace for they

49

always had just what she was looking for. Of course, apart from this there was also the close friendship they had formed over the years which was reason enough to go to the market.

"Is playing the guitar all it's hyped up to be?" she asked Sugar Cane after a short while.

He played on a little before answering. As she asked it he was taken back to the first man-to-man talk he could remember having with his father, David McCoy. At the time they were way up in the hills of Portland, picking out the mad weed from his father's ganja farm. He would never forget that day for it was also the first time he was actually taken to the sea of green shrubs his father used to talk about so much with his friends. For security reasons, the plantation was way out of the sight of civilization so the walk to get there had been a long one which exercised his thigh muscles like a series of squats. On the way up, Sugar Cane started wondering why on earth had he agreed to follow his father into this ...*bush* when he could have been spending his time more valuably hanging out at the Garlander. But then, when they finally made it to the top, all his reservations dissipated. It was just like David described it when talking with his friends, paradise. Only his father and company said it in terms of many enlightening smokes. Sugar Cane had seen it as a huge, sacred garden. Perhaps like the sort he would have expected to read about only in the Bible.

"Now you see why I cyaan' stop talkin' 'bout dis place," David had said to the younger Rastafarian, looking over the expanse of green, succulent shrubs that seemed to go all the way to the horizon. His eyes squinted against the sun and wind, his arms akimbo.

Sugar Cane nodded continuously for a while before saying, "Yes, Daddy, it's all it hype up to be."

" 'All it hype up to be?' " David had said as he walked off to do some more weeding. "No, it not. It look wonderful, but not all it hype up to be." He moved deeper into the plantation, so carefully the plants barely stirred as he went by them. "The only thing in this life that's all it hype up to be is pussy!" He had burst out laughing after saying this and Sugar Cane, suddenly feeling like a man, had laughed, too. But the teenaged virgin boy then wasn't sure exactly what his father had meant by this until a year and a half later when the girl next door gave him the full understanding one evening while her parents were away. He simply had to agree with his old man.

"'All it hype up to be?'" Sugar Cane turned to Sharon and mischievously thought of adding, *the only thing that's all it hype up to be is pussy...* but instead smiled and said, "I guess it depends on the individual." He played on a little longer. "It is a wonderful thing though. Relax you when you feelin' down an' make you forget your troubles for a while."

"Who taught you to play?" Sharon asked.

He shrugged. "Trial an' error. Bought I an' I first guitar when I was eighteen. But before that I an' I use to play-play with a old one I old man did have 'bout the house. So by the time I get my own I an' I was already playin' some tunes I use to hear on the radio. Still can't play by notes but that never slow I down yet."

"I've always wanted to play the guitar," Sharon said. "It just seems to have that magical sound that just... captivates me every time I hear it. Especially when it's playing reggae music. Just never been able to find time to take lessons."

"Well, I could teach you a thing or two if you like."

"You really would?" Her face lit up.

"Here," he said, stopped playing and handed the guitar to her. "We can start right now."

"No," she quickly declined, waving the spoon in one hand. She recoiled from the instrument as he gently thrust it at her. "I don't think I'd want to start wasting your time so soon."

"Stop worryin' 'bout my time an' seize the opportunity," he told her and rested it on her lap. He then relieved her of the spoon.

"You sure about this, Sugar Cane?"

He thought for a second then said, "Yes I sure ... Besides, I an' I *need* the extra cash."

"Extra money...?" she asked. "You mean you're *charging* me?"

"Gotcha!"

They both burst out laughing at the same time. Sharon's eyes squirted water. This was really a relief from the hectic day she'd had. Today she had visited the basic school to immunize students against measles, mumps and rubella. But before this the social worker part of her had taken Floyd Logan to visit Mitzy Harrison. Floyd was the sergeant at the Brown's Hall Police Station. He was the only one of Hector's bar buddies that she didn't mind talking to. The others were still a bit too boyish for her stomach.

Sharon had given it much thought this morning as she walked to work. The consequences, she knew, could prove unattractive for Angela and the rest of the girls. There was no telling just how Mitzy would act in a situation like this. "I just want you to talk to her," Sharon had told Floyd. "Just talk to her and let her stop doing this to her children." And this was really all she had wanted.

She certainly didn't want him to take her to court or any of that, for naturally this would be a disadvantage to the children. She never had to say this though for she knew that, being a man with children of his own, Floyd was quite capable of realising this himself. And besides, he was a community cop. He knew very well that the law was relative from town to town, and the smaller and more remote the town, the more relative the law that governed it. Back in Kingston, where he worked for a spell before being reassigned to Brown's Hall, he would have arrested a woman who merely thought of becoming a prostitute. Here in the hills however, things were sort of different. Sharlott had a little soliciting business going on with a few girls and Floyd knew this. Yet he turned a blind eye to it. *There were far worse things than prostitution,* he sometimes thought, *all I need to know is that the girls are in fact women.* And besides, people here—men and women— thought Sharlott's services were very important, for there were grown men walking around who would still be virgins if it wasn't for Sharlott and the Barn Yard Girls. And if they wouldn't be virgins they'd be rapists or—what did they call them up here?— donkey men!

Sharon had to assume that it was the presence of the man in the police uniform that got to Mitzy. When they arrived and Mitzy saw them, she was silent as a stadium with everybody gone. And when Officer Logan warned her in his long-arm-of-the-law tone she actually cringed as he spoke. Sharon was baffled by the sudden change in attitude. No *a yuh did puuush dem out,* or any of that. And when Floyd concluded by saying, "Now rememba, a warn yuh! If yuh mek this sort of thing happen again!" wagging his index finger in front of her like a confused speedometer dial, "Alright ma'am?"

53

"Yes Offisah!" just barely escaped Mitzy Harrison's lips.

As Floyd took Sharon back to the clinic she'd said, "I don't know how you do it."

"All I did is mention the words *courts, law,* and *jailhouse.* Nobody want their name and those words in the same sentence," he told her.

The guitar seemed much larger sitting in her lap than it did when Sugar Cane had it. Awkwardly she held it with both hands to prevent it from toppling over. He leaned over, assisting her by correctly placing her hands on the neck and box. And by the time she had stopped laughing he was familiarizing her with the possible sounds of each string. She listened as he spoke and showed much initial interest. It was obvious to him though that this was going to be a real task for she really didn't know much when it came to music. But at least at the end of the half hour he allowed her, she was still full of enthusiasm.

"Where is he?" Sharon asked, handing the guitar back to Sugar Cane. She passed it on with as much care as one would a baby. He relieved her of it in the same way.

"Where's who?"

"Your old man." She took the spoon. "Where is he now?"

"Dead," he answered frankly. "Both I parents are. Mother died of breast cancer from I an' I was just startin' St. Jago High. Government say I ol' man wasn't farmin' exactly what them want him to, so them prison him. Contracted pneumonia. Never survived it."

"I'm sorry..."

"Me too, sister Sharon, but that's life." He picked a few strings as if he really didn't want to talk about this anymore.

Realising this, Sharon brain stormed for something else to say. "So what do you think of Brown's Hall?"

"The women seem very nice," he answered grinning. "The man them I not so sure 'bout. An' apart from what I see from the bus I really haven't seen much of the place itself."

"Not much to see," she admitted. "But unlike Kingston or even Spanish Town, it's quite peaceful. I like that. The way of life you might find a bit too slow most of the times as there's really nothing to do except maybe go over by Tony's to have a beer, listen to the juke. If you weren't the pub-going type and you didn't go to church you simply have no choice but to go to bed."

"Are you the pub-goin' type?" Sugar Cane asked.

She sighed. "I'm afraid not... And I only go to church on new year's eve." *I don't go more often because I think the pastor is sick in his head,* she thought but said nothing. Pastor Granstan Miller was as holy rolling and full of life as they came. But he also had a way of bringing his point across which Sharon thought was unbecoming of a pastor. Right now she could clearly remember an instance at the last new year's eve's service she attended. Granstan was at the pew, sapping sweat from his face with a perfectly white handkerchief. He had backed off his jacket some time earlier and was now sporting his sky blue shirt with the sleeves rolled up to the elbows and his tie loose about his neck. "Brothers an' sisters, I think Jesus is a John Crow," he barfed into the microphone. It sounded more like, *brodas an' sistas I tink jeesas is a jangcro.* "You hear what a say?" he shouted at the congregation and thumped his fist on the pew. "A say, I *tink jeesas is a jangcro!* You know why?" There was a hush over the church as everybody waited to hear just how he was going to justify equating Jesus with a scavenger. Even Deacon Elroy Williams who would always be shouting, "Tell it like it is, pastor. Hallelujah! Bless God, bless God!" was totally still. If Deacon Williams were a man of the world, the expression Sharon noticed on his face at that moment would have read, *what the fuck is Granstan sayin'?* But he was a man of God so it was only right for Sharon to assume that his thoughts were more like, *Lord forgive me, but what the fuck is Granstan sayin'?*

"A say, do you want to know why a say jeesas is a jangcro?" the pastor had asked again, his eyes darting over the many faces that stared uncomprehendingly back at him. At this point everybody, including Sharon, shouted a resounding, "Yes!" Pastor Granstan Miller had smiled then. "Jeesus is a jangcro for when I was a dead meat he flew down from heaven and picked me up. Can I hear a Amen?"

Amen!

"So I guess that put you in the bed-by-dusk category?" Sugar Cane said.

"Pretty much," she replied.

It was now Sugar Cane's turn to leave the conversation hanging. And with the eagerness of an imp, started playing the guitar again. "I an' I goin' to sing you a song," he told her.

She smiled and said nothing as he found a tune unfamiliar to her ears. It was now just going on the down side of six o'clock.

The air was starting to get chilly and all around you could hear few crickets beginning to chirp. The sun itself was a fading orange glow in the west.

The song Sugar Cane did for her was Never Say Die, belting out the notes with even more energy than he had back at Jamtouch. His timber voice made her quiver visibly and her eyes welled with warm tears. By the second singing of the bridge she was joining in. Sugar Cane enjoyed the sound of this greatly. It was a wonderful feeling being able to touch somebody with your song like this. Maybe not all it was hyped up to be—but wonderful anyway.

"That was beautiful," she said after he had reverberated the last notes. "Thanks."

He thought of telling her the history of this song. That he had written it and how it was rejected by the producer today. The urge to just let it all out on somebody else was strong but he managed to contain himself. Maybe some other time. He didn't want to risk stirring up feelings which Jah-Jah Son's support had managed to suppress.

And to be certain she didn't get the chance to even start thinking of asking him about the song, he quickly ran on to another number. It was Bob Marley's *No Woman No Cry*. She applauded this one with an ecstatic scream and kicking legs. As best she could manage the notes she tried to sing along. A lock fell to Sugar Cane's face as he bobbed his head to the tune. Sharon, while rocking with him, used a hand to comb it back. She liked the way it felt to her touch, full and strong. He liked the way her gentle touch felt against his forehead. Again he missed a note but this time she didn't notice.

"Turn your lights down low," Sugar Cane continued the medley with another Bob Marley hit.

"And pull your window curtain," Sharon joined in. She was a real fan of Marley he gathered.

At the moment the red Volkswagen pulled up at the gate with Hector, Sharon and Sugar Cane were looking at each other with radiant grins, rocking to the tune as they sang, *"I wanna give you some love. I wanna give you some good good lovin'."*

CHAPTER SIX

"I JUST can't feel good goin' home anymore," Hector said with a grave sigh. He was in the passenger seat of Ken Jackson's Bug. The red car was now about a half a mile away from the school and one mile and a half from Brown's Hall Crossroads. The narrow, two-way road they drove on was flanked on both sides with small coffee and cocoa farms. It was the first Hector was saying anything since Ken offered him a ride home.

"I hate to say this," Ken said, "but I fuckin' told you a thousand times." On an Agricultural Sciences teacher's salary the Volkswagen was the closest Ken would probably ever come to purchasing the Porsche he so badly desired. The Bug was a pretty reliable point-A-to-point-B car that didn't leave him stranded even when the roads were flooded. But the Porsche, he gathered, got you all that... plus girls! The only girls Bugs got you were the ones Ken referred to as *skets. Girls you can usually get after takin' them to Burger King or Kentucky Fried Chicken,* he often thought. The Porsche, on the other hand, could get you some super model type babes. "This one-woman thing for ever an' ever won't work!" Ken continued. "What happen when you put a nice, juicy piece of beef in your mouth an' chew on it for too long? It get fresh an' stringy! Same thing with woman. This one-woman thing only lead to the death of manhood." He swerved to avoid a patch of potholes.

Hector said nothing to this. He really didn't hear much of what Ken was saying for he was deep in thought. Today he had almost told a student to *go fuck himself.* At the time he had been trying to get the concept of completing the squares through their skulls, but as he had expected it just wasn't working. And when he asked, "You understand?" the class had just stared at him in their usual lame blankness as if they had no idea at all of just what Hector was doing at the black board, his hands powdered with chalk dust. So he had asked again, "Students, do you understand what I'm sayin' to you?" And as he said this he counted *two* in his mind. It was his style to ask them three times and if they didn't answer he would then say, "Alright, case closed." Then he would move on to the other aspect of the topic.

But it never got that far this time for as he was about to ask for the third and final time a student in the back—Ricardo Durrant—called out, "Sir, I never-ever understan' nothin' dat you teach." The boy's voice quivered as he spoke but what he had said was clear enough for everyone to hear. The look on Ricardo's face at the moment said that he wished he could have withdrawn the words but they were already out and they were out for good. Ricardo rubbed the sweat from his palms into his khaki pants.

"So you don't think there's a reason for that?" Hector had asked. Thirty-two pairs of eyes followed the exchange. Angela Harrison was in the front row, just in front of Hector's gut. She could feel the desk shake when Hector spoke to Ricardo and it frightened her. But even as she sat there sweating beneath the blue tunic, she was thinking, *yes, Ricardo; finally somebody's sayin' it to him. Finally!* At the time she was thinking this, Sharon was taking the police to have the little talk with Mitzy Harrison.

"Yes, sir," Ricardo answered. He was much more relaxed now and his voice was as loud as Hector's. It was as if he had been planning to say this since the start of the school year and only now thought that he was really ready. He had startled his classmates, for most of them had never really heard him say more than a word or two under his breath. Some students from other classes quite frequently asked if he was dumb for they had never heard him speak or seen him in a conversation. So now that he had taken it upon himself to be the spokesperson for the class, they were truly startled. The good thing though, was that they could see that he had startled Mr White, too.

"What is the reason?" Hector shouted at the boy. The class recoiled as if from anticipating a blow. *"What is it?"* Hector came forward to meet Ricardo's answer halfway down the aisle.

Ricardo sat there, his eyes watery and bloodshot—but he wasn't crying. He glanced at the faces around him, trying to gather data. He sheered his palms on his pants again.

"Answer me!" Hector commanded. "What is the rea–"

"Sir, you can't teach!" Ricardo shouted back at him.

"Can't teach?" Hector had whispered. It was as if Ricardo had used a totally different language now and Hector was trying to work out a proper translation. "What do you know about teachin'? Do you know that the first year I came to this place the pass rate for mathematics at this school jumped from forty to seventy-five percent? Did you know that?"

"No sir," Ricardo answered and then added, "...But that was donkey years ago. We talkin' 'bout *now*. You can't teach *now*."

"Listen to me boy, why don't you go *fff-*" Hector stopped himself from going further but he was quite sure the class had an idea of what he had attempted to say. This had never happened to him before. Profanities were always reserved for home and when he was with the boys over by Tony's. He had never even used them when he was in the staff room after school playing dominoes. School was a place you just didn't fuck with in that sort of way. The incident made him ask himself many questions. Top of the list were, *am I really losin' it as a teacher? And if so, why?*

And now as he sat here, the wind slapping sense into him, he thought he had the answer. He had met Sharon five years ago at a career expo where she was giving free blood pressure checks. Back then, he had just finished his diploma at Mico and Sharon was doing her last year at the nursing school. He could remember thinking, *Fuck!, I'm in love,* when he caught her eyes as she took his arm to wrap the black sphygmomanometer cuff round it. And when he thought this he was almost sure that every man who had come and seen her sitting there in her candy stripes had thought the very same thing. She had been that beautiful. So when he gave her his number and begged her to call him as soon as she got off, he really wasn't expecting her to. For one, he was a teacher and that meant that your clothes didn't look as attractive as the guys who worked in the corporate world. Also, he was certain she had seen him catch the bus home—no car. And finally, they didn't call him *Captain Cave Man* back in his freshman year for nothing. It wasn't that he was ugly why he got the name, for back at Mico College all freshmen for some reason or the other were regarded as ugly. It was more the fact that he had a naturally gruff voice and the seniors had realised this from the very first time they asked him his name. So they had pinned the nickname on him and for the first two weeks of his freshman year Hector had to rise at four every morning and shout, *'CAPTAIN CAVE MAAAAAAN! UNGA MUNGA!!!"* And two hours later he was obliged to say, *"SIX O' THE CLOCK AND ALL IS WE-ELL."* The image had worked wonders for him throughout the rest of college though for all he had to say was, *"Unga Munga"* and the girls would just go crazy. He did it so often till after a time he actually sounded like the real captain Cave Man and he had started to really like it, too. But the mere sight of Sharon had made him think whether he needed to tone down a bit. And as he spoke to her that day he was thinking, *I'm sinkin' myself with every word I say. My voice alone is goin' to make her think I'm a crusty and she'll just take my number and put it in the bin when I'm gone. She'll take it 'cause she's scared of what I might do if she doesn't. She won't call me.*

But Sharon did call him as soon as she got off that day. About six or so months later he asked her why him when so many other men with cars and well grooming must have made advances. "I like your voice," she had answered, "Sounds so...masculine." When Hector heard this, all he could say was, *"Unga munga!"*

This was the beginning of what they had hoped to be a long time of smiles. And for a time it was. He could remember climbing over the fence of the nurses' home at desperate hours of night as he snuck in to see her and sometimes ripping his pants as he snuck himself back out. The first time she had telephoned her parents to introduce him her mother was asking him questions like what were his plans for the future, while her father was telling him that if he forced his daughter to join any bad companies *"over there I'll personally fly over and shoot you." (Shoot you mumma!)* Hector had thought of saying then but this was also one of the rare occasions when he thought it best not to say what was on his mind. And how could he forget those grand plans they had to get married someday and have a few kids.

Hector came to realise, however, that things changed as time moved on. His dream of settling down and starting a family wasn't looking so much like the best thing after all. And especially so that he had come to realise that she quite likely wasn't going to be having any children and was trying to trick him into staying with her anyway. Maybe she wanted them to adopt a few kids. *She can screw that idea!* Or maybe she just wanted them to stay together alone for eternity. Whatever it was that she was selling he just wasn't interested in buying anymore. People had a right to change their minds and he had changed his. Hector wanted out of this deal. He had been wanting to say this to her for some time now but just hadn't figured out how. This was one instance that he had to admit that his *call a spade a spade* approach just wasn't going to work. It was like every time he felt like he was ready to tell her, his brain just got clogged and he simply couldn't do it. Eventually, though, he knew it had to be done.

Staying was only making him more and more miserable as time passed. If there was really a problem with his teaching then this was what was causing it. The dream had died and he was still living in it. If he remained, he thought, it wouldn't only kill his ability to teach, but it would probably kill him too.

Ken honked the horn as he navigated a corner. "Monogamy," he went and kissed his teeth, "Fart that!"

Hector caught on to that part. "How you know that's my problem? It couldn't be somethin' else?"

"Somethin' else?" Ken asked. "The only thing that can make a man as distressed as you are when he thinks of goin' home is the woman he's livin' with. I see the look in you guys faces all the while and say to myself, no matter how much a woman wants me to live with her I won't allow myself to fall into the trap. Mi? Not a rass a dat!" Ken Jackson was six feet tall, tan complexion with black hair and dark eyes that made his female students swoon when he looked at them. He took pride in knowing that at thirty-five he could still do this to teenagers but remained grounded enough not to allow their very mature advances to get him sleeping with them. "Check me in another three years," he would sometimes say if the girl in question seemed a potentially good catch. The female teachers, however, were mature and legally capable of making their own decisions. Ken took full advantage of this for they too swooned when he gave them *that* look. He respected the vows of married people so he didn't usually come on to married women—but if they made the advance he wasn't going to turn it down. *After all,* he would think, *I'm sexy, not stupid.* As a rule he didn't make passes at his friends' women either. So even as he thought he would eat Sharon's cunt any day now he would never say it for she was Hector's woman. If she once gave him the hint that she wanted it too, however, that was a different matter altogether. The problem was, she had never given him a second look as if she might just be interested some day... even a few years from now. In fact, he got the impression that she didn't really like him much.

If Sharon didn't like him she wasn't the only one. Paul Frater didn't like him much either. Ken was the reason Hector had never seen Frater at Tony's. Back in November of '91, Ken Jackson made Paul Frater do something he had never done in all his forty-six years. But then, when he did it, no one was a bit surprised. The consensus was not that they expected Frater to go around breaking people's noses but that Ken had it coming. "You jus' don' do things like dat!" Tony had told Hector once as he related the incident. "You just don' fool around with a man's daughter an' come brag about it to his face in public. You jus' don' do dat!" And especially so when the man's daughter was thought of in the community as a goodly Christian lady. *You jus' don' do dat!*

But Ken didn't know this. Either that or it had slipped his memory. They were all at Tony's sipping beer and making jokes as usual. Frater had only just told him that he screwed around so much because he had to. "No woman nuh want to experience your poor excuse for performance a second time," Frater had told him, "so every time you want a dose you have to go beg some-body new." They were all a bit tipsy so they found this very funny and laughed excessively. Then Ken got up from his stool and said, "Well, Cheryl get it every week and she seem to love it." When he said that it caused a hush over the small gathering. It was the first that anybody—including Paul Frater—learnt that Deaconess Cheryl Frater was secretly visiting Ken. Maybe Ken should have stopped there but he didn't. "So me storm the meat so she rail up," Ken had continued, "So me storm it, so she rail u–"

The older man's fist had connected with the nose so quickly and with such a force Ken was sent reeling to the red tiles, his mouth agape and his eyes watering. Seconds later a bleeding from his nostrils. Ken got up in a bull charge as he shouted, "What the fuck was that for?" He had rammed Frater in the gut. That was when Frater held onto the gold cross Ken had in his ear and yanked it out causing more blood to spill. The fight would have continued had the other guys not rushed to part them after allowing Ken to get what they thought he deserved. Frater had simply walked out of the bar that night and never visited again. On his way out he had said, "What am I doin' here? You could all be my children!"

Ken didn't wear that cross in his ear these days. The horrifying thoughts of it being yanked out again just couldn't leave his mind. The space was now occupied by a gold knob one of his students had bought him as a Christmas gift last December. She was one of the girls he had asked to check him in three years. Cheryl Frater had since migrated to Canada where she got married to a Baptist minister. She came out every now and then to look for her parents but when she did she didn't see Ken. Some people said Paul Frater forbade her from ever going near Ken Jackson again. Ken thought she stayed away because she couldn't resist the temptation if he came too close.

"So," Hector went after allowing what Ken had just said to soak into his system, "you suggestin' that I should leave her?"

"No, I'm not suggestin' anythin' here," Ken said. "If you want to leave her it's up to you. But considerin' that you two have gone what, four, five years? I don't think you should take it that far."

"Alright," Hector said, "I know you're not suggestin' anythin' but how far you think I should take it then?"

"Fool around a little," Ken told him. "Put back some fire inna yuh wire. You know how much woman in Brown's Hall would want to test you out? Not to mention some of the teachers back at school."

"You think so ?"

"How you mean if I think so? I know so. Take the librarian, Miss Peddie, for example. Every mornin' her father drop her off and pick her up in the evenin's. Guess why? She nuh have nuh man! 'Bout thirty to-rass and she sits there with her rosy self sayin' she is virgin."

"She's a virgin?" Hector asked.

"So she say when I asked her. Give you a joke, earlier on this year they had a guidance session in the library. When the counselor started talkin' bout safe sex and took out a sample condom Miss Peddie shout out, *'Is that name so?'* We couldn't help but laugh."

"Is that name so?" Hector jeered and laughed.

"Is that name so!" Ken repeated, letting go of the steering wheel for a second to open his palms to the heavens in a quizzical gesture. "In this year 1996 woman never seen condom before. Can you imagine that?"

"That's sad though, eh?" Hector said.

"It's sad yes! That's why I want you to hold her rass after school one evenin' right there inna the library mek she know what she missin'. I beg her all the while but she's not givin' me. Says I'm too wild, and –" Ken adjusted his voice to sound feminine, "–'What I want is a man who will love and cherish me for ever and ever. All you want is fornication.'"

"But I wouldn't want to love and cherish her either," Hector said.

"True, but she doesn't know that. She thinks you're the deep, sensitive sort of man with good values. You can always fool her up and she'll believe. No matter what I tell her she won't believe for she's heard 'bout me."

Hector thought for a while. "It sounds good," he said. "But doin' that sort of thing is not as easy as you might think, you know. I think it's easier for me to just tell her it's all over and God knows that's not easy at all."

"It's as easy as you make it, Hector, it's as easy as you make it. Personally I think you would hurt her less if you fool around than if you tell her it's over. If you were a single man like me I'd say don't get hooked up with anybody, stay single an' run road. It so happens that you are hooked and that means another person's feelin's are at stake. But then, like I said, I'm not suggestin' anythin'. I'm just tellin' you what I feel."

The car slowly drove up to Hector's gate and stopped. Hector got his things from the back seat and opened the door. This was when he saw Sharon and the beast under the ackee tree singing away.

"But what is this?" Ken said, as if to himself, and chuckled. "Now I know what them mean when them say *some man run yard an' some man run 'round yard!*" He honked the horn and when Sharon looked up he waved to her. She waved back, still singing.

"What the fuck's that supposed to mean now, Ken?" Hector asked as he got out of the car, balancing three hard-cover math texts in his left hand.

"You don't know?" Ken went. "Alright, later we'll talk 'bout this one, Hector. You know you can't get away from this one." Ken Jackson honked his horn once more and in a moment the fire-engine-red Volkswagen was zooming away from the cross-roads like the scene at the end of a movie.

"Want to come join us, Hector?" Sharon asked as Hector came into the yard. "It's real fun."

Hector peered at her real good for a moment then kissed his teeth in a most resentful manner as he walked past them. "Think I have fuckin' time to waste," he said.

When Hector got to the bedroom, he rested the texts on the dresser and changed into a T-shirt which he found more comfort-able than the long sleeved shirts he had to wear to work. He then put the shirt he had taken off into the laundry bag for Mrs. Bailey to pick up on the weekend. That was if she decided to come, he thought, for she had a way of just falling ill every other weekend. He had threatened to fire her once or twice but Sharon had asked him not to for Mrs. Bailey needed the money. She was an elderly widow who had to support herself and Lipton, the seventeen year old son of her daughter who had left for Miami over ten years now to find a better life but never been heard from since. A real sad story if there ever was one, Hector sometimes thought, but it worked on Sharon's heart enough for her to want to excuse the old lady's no-show habits. In a way, he guessed, the story had worked on him, too.

Hector came out to the kitchen only to discover that dinner hadn't been served yet. The meal was still in shiny steel pots on the stove top while the celebration continued outside.

It's as easy as you make it, he could remember Ken telling him. Hector tried to think straight as he started short-pacing the kitchen. Here he was, home from a hard day's work and as hungry as Oliver Twist. There she was under the ackee tree merry-making with the beast. Why was he allowing this? And she had the nerve to ask him to come join them! *Why am I allowin' this???*

Because some man run yard an' some man run 'round yard, perhaps? a voice asked back.

"Fuck that!" Hector said and started out of the kitchen. He went to the living room window, stuck his head out and hollered, "What about the food?"

The guitar stopped. Sharon sprang up, startled by the sudden outcry. "Oh gosh ... totally forgot."

You didn't forget shit, Hector thought. *You just don't give a fuck anymore. But I tell you, you aren't the only one.*

It's as easy as you make it.

He watched her hurry to the kitchen while he kicked his shoes off and threw himself on the sofa. In a while he could smell meat balls being heated up. He found the remote under the cushion and checked the TV but there was nothing on so he turned it back off. Hector stretched himself out on the sofa and stared at the ceiling as he waited.

It's as easy as you make it!

"Dinner's ready," Sharon called as she left him to eat while she went to have a bath.

***

Sugar Cane came out to sit by his back door step just about the same moment Sharon came out to pin some things on the clothes line. He had gone inside after Sharon had left to go prepare Hector's dinner and had, until now, been at his desk working on a song which had come into his mind while he was under the ackee tree. *Let Jah Lead,* he titled it. He had reached the end of the first verse when he started having a song writer's block so he decided to come out to the back yard where he could enjoy some of the cool breeze and have an inspiring smoke. He wasn't expecting to see Sharon when he came out but there she was. She must have just had a bath he thought, for she was wearing only a sky blue towel wrapped about her. The towel fitted her like a tight mini dress, revealing her well toned thighs which had the same even cocoa butter brown of her face and arms, and the part of her back that he could now see. Sharon first pinned her wash rag on the line and then pink panties so petite it reminded Sugar Cane of a rose petal. Maybe she isn't even wearin' any now, Sugar Cane thought. But then he would never know this for he wasn't her man; Hector White was. He couldn't help but wondering what he would do if he were in Hector's place right now. He would wait until she got back inside, then he'd sneak up on her from behind and–

Sharon turned to go back inside to Hector. She smiled insecurely as she saw him sitting there... *watching her.* He just knew that she could tell what he was thinking when she saw his eyes. Those thoughts always came out in your eyes whether you wanted them to or not. He didn't like this for these thoughts were wrong. The best thing to do now, he thought, was to go back inside and banish these thoughts from his mind. The only problem was he couldn't move. Not just yet! Not until Sharon was totally out of sight. Not until he had seen the last of her tight ass going through the door. Just a day and a half of being here and already the woman was doing this to him. What would he be thinking after three months? What would he be thinking *tomorrow?*

As soon as she went inside, Sugar Cane got up and returned to his desk. He took up the legal pad and pencil but his mind was even more blocked now than it had been when he went out to clear it. Only now, it was the picture of Sharon smiling at him as the thought of having her filled his mind.

Quickly he put the pencil and paper away and took up the Bible he had there on his desk. He had to get her out of his mind, he was thinking—*had to!*

It was his intention to simply open the Bible and read the first chapter that his eyes fell on. It was something he did whenever he found that life's temptations were getting to him in a way he thought he couldn't manage all alone. Sometimes it seemed to work, sometimes it didn't—but then it was never a waste of time to read the Bible.

The fact that when the book came open his eyes fell on Exodus chapter 20 didn't bother him. In fact, he relished reading from Exodus; it was a book that gave him hope and will to move on. What bothered him to the point where he literally felt himself tremble, though, was the particular verse his consciousness zeroed in on.

> *Thou shalt not covet thy neighbour's house*
> *Thou shalt not covet thy neighbour's wife, nor*
> *his manservant, nor his maidservant, nor his ox,*
> *nor his ass, nor any thing that is thy neighbour's.*

73

It was verse 17 and it cut through him so hard his head hurt.

Thou shalt not covet thy neighbour's wife!

No sooner than he read it Sugar Cane fell to his knees praying. "Jah!" he said. "I beg you, forgive me of my terrible sins against thy words. Jah know that I an' I am human an' am liable to sin from time to time as temptation rides I an' I like I am a mule for the Babylonians. But I an' I know that, Jah! Selassie – I will deliver I an' I just as you delivered Daniel from the den of lions. Jah Selassie—I! Ever livin', ever faithful, ever sure! Deliver I an ' I oh Jah! Deliver." His words were high pitched and followed in rapid succession, making it all sound like a sacred rap. He held the Bible clasped in his hands so firmly veins stood out on his arms like wisps crawling up a tree. Eyes shut so tightly they squirted water as he bled his heart out before Selassie.

This is a sign an' a half, he kept thinking to himself even as he prayed. *This was a sign that Selassie was still guidin' I an' I when I fall weak of faith.* When his world was falling apart all around him, Selassie was still there helping him through. It was comforting to know this. "Oh Jah! Oh Jah! Oh Jah!" he began again. "Oh Jah! Oh Jah! Oh J–"

"–Oh man!" Hector called from the other side of the wall. "Stop that rass noise so I can have some peace and quiet. I hope this thing is not a daily ritual!"

Sugar Cane didn't answer. Just another stumbling block in the way of righteousness, he thought and smiled understandingly to himself. He prayed more silently now and as he did this thought, *If Mr. Hector White knew why I an' I am prayin' he'd want me to do it every single minute for as long as I live in this place.*

CHAPTER SEVEN

"KEN, WHAT is the difference between a donkey's backside an' a mail box?" Floyd Logan asked from his swivel-stool.

Ken thought hard for a long while before answering, "I don't have a clue."

"That means if I ask you to post my letter you may very well push it up a donkey's backside!' Floyd returned wittily and Tony's Bar was ablaze with laughter. This was usually what the atmosphere was like when the gang got together.

It was during this fit of laughter that Hector walked in, cotching on the first vacant stool in sight.

Tony, a burly man who wore steel-rim bifocals, passed him a beer from the other side of the counter.

Hector still hadn't caught onto what they were laughing about when he decided to join in. There was a TV perched on a rack in the far corner. WCW was on but the volume was down to a minimum. Ray Charles', *You Don't Know Me* was on the juke. And if it wasn't Ray it would have been a number by Jim Reeves, Percy Sledge or King Elvis. These were the guys Floyd's monopoly over the juke dictated every night he came by—every fucking night he came by.

"But speakin' of backsides," Ken said at length, "Hector, is what kind of backside that I saw happenin' over by your place there today?" He gulped rum from a heavy bottom glass and grinned teasingly as he spoke. "Floyd, if I tell you what I saw you'd probably have a heart attack and it has nothin' to do with you."

"Tell me anyway," Floyd said, "We all must go some time."

"Tony, what do you say?"

"Talk you tale, Kenny boy," Tony went as he sponged glass sweat from the linoleum counter top.

"Well alright." And with this Ken told them all he had seen and heard as he dropped Hector off today. Hector didn't once try to stop him. There wasn't a soul in this small room who had never been the butt of an embarrassing joke at some time or the other. It was a medicine they all had to take.

"A rastaman?" Tony went.

"Of all the people in the fuckin' world, eh Tony?" Hector said. "I don't know why Frater put one of those to live under the same roof with a decent citizen like me."

"'Tis because you won't drop Ken's company," Floyd said and chuckled. "You know the man don't like a bone in Ken Jackson an' still you givin' Ken reason to stop at his gate."

"And if you don't watch it that rastaman goin' to do more than just live there wit you," Ken added.

"Singin' love songs to Sharon!—And Bob Marley love songs at that! Any man who wants a woman badly enough only have to sing one or two Bob Marley love songs to her. She gone to him," Floyd coughed up bubbles of laughter.

"And he can play the guitar too, you know," Ken added. "You should see how well him can pluck those strings."

"So you know dat when him ready to pluck di G-String him know exactly what to do."

"You know the thing, Tony," Floyd said.

Hector laughed along with them for he knew it was all said in the spirit of the moment. "Personally," he said, "I don't mind if he takes her. Thinkin' of callin' it quits anyway." He sipped his beer and stared across the bar at the TV—not really watching it though, just staring.

"You don't mean that," Floyd told him.

"He does," Ken said. "Can't you see he's a fuckin loser? The rastaman hasn't even tried anythin' yet and already he's givin' up. Loser!"

"And who's better to tell us about losers than you, Ken?" Hector asked. "You've been losin' so long you actually think you're ahead of everybody else!"

"But I am," Ken told him with a smart smile.

Hector threw his hands above his head in a hopeless gesture. "Same fuckin' thing!" He sent nods to Tony and Floyd. "What did I tell you?"

"You don't think I'm ahead of the pack?" Ken went in mock disbelief. "I have girls fallin' at my feet. And any time they not fallin' as I'd want them to all I need is two hundred dollars and I can have a different woman for every night of the week. Floyd you're a policeman so you know what I'm talkin' 'bout."

"Because I'm a policeman?" Floyd asked.

"Yeah!" Ken said. "Every policeman buy whore just as how every policeman nyam pussy. It's a given."

"No Ken," Floyd said, "you can't generalise like that. That not true at all."

"What? You sayin' there are some policeman who don't eat cunt?"

"That's not the part I'm talkin' 'bout, dummy," Floyd was quick to clarify. "It's the part 'bout the whores. I don't buy whores. Never have, never will. I've been married twenty years now an' I won't say I've never lusted, but that's as far as it will go. I know how much my relationship with my wife means to me."

"So what were you doin' up at Sharlott's last week Friday night?"

"Is de same reason why Frater bus' you' rass nose! You chat too much sometimes," Floyd returned and chuckled, then on a more serious note added, "I went up there in response to a call that she was hearin' strange noises after hours."

"But 'is a whore house! What else she expect to hear?" It was Tony. They all laughed.

Ken said, "So what you sayin', Floyd, you'll never buy a piece if the need arises?"

"No. What I'm sayin' is that the need will never arise. For one, I'm a married man, and two, the risk of gettin' HIV an' other diseases just too great."

"That might be true," Ken said, "But I use my rubbers every time. And I don't have to worry about rastaman wooin' my woman. I sleep well at night, believe me."

"It mus' be hard seein' a Rasta in the same yard with you though," Tony said, "knowin' how you feel 'bout them."

"It's as hard as it gets," Hector went, shaking his head. "It's as bad as it gets."

Floyd said on a seemingly more sober note, "It could be worse."

"What's worse than that?" Hector asked.

"I don't know." Floyd shrugged. "...Livin' with two Rastas perhaps." Of course they all found this quite laughable. Floyd continued, "In all seriousness though, Rastafarianism is just another way of life an', personally, I don't have a problem with it. As a matter of fact, I sometimes wonder if I wouldn't feel more comfortable as a person if I worshiped a god that had my colour. Why should a black man keep a white or Jewish picture of God in his house?"

"But they worship Selassie," Hector said. "Selassie was just another man, how could they call him God?"

"Hindu worship cattle; you don't hear everybody makin' a fuss about that." Floyd paused for a drink. His reflection in the mirror on the other side of the counter reminded him of just how tired he was. "Out here we use cattle to make hamburgers an' cod soup."

"Well, I guess you have a point if you look at it that way," Hector said. "But that doesn't change the price of rice in China. I can't see why they have to wear that bundle of dirty hair on their heads either."

"So it's just the hair that really givin' you a problem?"

"Well it doesn't help, Floyd, I can say that much."

79

"What if it's a clean locks, would that make a difference?" Floyd asked.

Hector sipped beer and thought. "Not really, locks is locks, dirty or clean."

"Maybe it's because you growing up goin' to the barber shop every time your hair got quarter inch off your scalp why you feel this way," Floyd suggested. He took a long refreshing drink of the beer Tony had slipped into his hand. "So you just grow up thinkin' the barber and him craft represent what's pure and anyone who don't subscribe to that belief is unpure and should be scorned like a leper."

"Damn right about that," Hector said.

"But then you must be able to figure out that low hair don't always mean *clean* hair—and neither does long hair. Not because someone's hair is short mean that he's pure. Quite a number of men with short hair are very far from pure in thoughts and deeds. This I know *especially* because I'm a cop."

"But rastaman do bad things, too," Hector argued.

"True," Floyd agreed. "The same is true for Christians and Jews and Buddhists and Hindu and any other that they may have goin' on out there. Some bad, some tryin' to live a honest life."

"Moses saw the promised land but never reached there," Ken interrupted mockingly.

Hector said, "I see what you're sayin', Floyd, but that–"

"–Don't change the price of rice in China. It can sure change it in Jamaica though and that's where we are right now. All I'm sayin' is, in this world we have good people and bad people. Wearin' locks doesn't always mean you're good but wearing it doesn't always mean you're bad, either. As far as I see it's a people thing. Everybody deserve a fair trial, give him one."

"That's why them move you from Kingston," Ken said. "You too just! Where you ever hear of a just police officer? 'Bout *it's a people thing.* Big speech, win any election with that. But I want to see you go on a raid down town Kingston and see if that *it's a people thing* don't backfire on you."

Tony and Floyd chuckled, Hector on the other hand was silent and pensive. After a short while Hector said, "Well I don't give a fuck which rastaman bad or which one good. All I know, I don't like none of them."

***

In another hour and a half and a few idle talks of whatever else came to their heads they were ready to retire to their homes. Tony saw them all out then pushed the big double doors shut. The lights went out but not before those of Ken's bug and Floyd Logan's police trooper came on. Both guys honked their horns to Hector as they drove away. He waved at them and crossed the street. It was quite chilly tonight, he realised, now that he was out of the warmth of the bar. And it was only going to get colder as December approached. Colder to the point where even people who came from England to visit their relatives for Christmas would find it pretty cold, too. Hector could do without the cold. It made his ears ache sometimes when it got really bad, and the house didn't have a water heater so getting up to bathe in the mornings could become a real terror.

Hector rubbed his palms and then stuck them in his pockets as he came into the yard. He walked briskly with his shoulders hooked up to his ears. The beast, he saw, was sprawled out in one of the plastic chairs on the veranda. And he was smoking something. Hector reminded himself to disinfect those chairs whenever he was going to sit in them but then thought that that probably would be taking things a little too far. After all, it really wasn't leprosy was it? As he came up to the steps he realised that the beast wasn't wearing any shirt. The stoplight which floated just in front of his lips got brighter as he pulled on what Hector's sense of smell now confirmed to be a joint. Hector thought back to the conversation they had at Tony's not long ago and was convinced that if he had remembered to mention the fact that ganja smoking was illegal yet Rastafarians used it in worship or any other time they damn well pleased, he would have gained some more logical points to support his views. Then again, he thought, maybe not. To his knowledge the police in Brown's Hall had never ever arrested anybody found cultivating or possessing ganja. Yet most of the farmers here planted a little to supplement their income. Everybody knew about it—even Floyd—but nobody said anything because this was Brown's Hall and the laws were different up here. Up here the only crimes that mattered were killings, rapes, stealings, use of hard drugs like cocaine and the attempts to do these things. All else more or less got a blind eye. *No wonder It came here to live,* Hector thought, *this place is like a fuckin' haven for guys like him.* As Hector thought, though, he concluded that Floyd was right about one thing; everyone deserved an equal chance in the social world. *And besides,* he thought, *it's only wise to try and know your enemy as much as possible.* So instead of beating the chilling wind to get inside Hector sat in the next chair. It was a real challenge to endure the cold but he figured that if this beast could do it without shirt he should be able to do it also—even if he had to keep his shirt on.

"You not cold?" Hector asked.

"What you talkin' 'bout brother? Course not! Is hot I an' I feel hot why I come out here. Inside the room there's like a furnance."

"It's that ball of fire you're smokin' that causin' the heat. Don't know why you people have to do that shit anyway."

"Source of comfort and inspiration, brother." Sugar Cane took another pull and nodded, satisfied.

Hector rubbed his palms again and then realised he had actually done so. He hoped he wasn't portraying the image of the–

(some man run yard an' some man run 'round yard!)

–weaker man by doing this. But then the other wasn't a man, he was a fucking animal! He was *supposed* to be better at things like this.

"Source of madness, too," Hector went with a grunt.

"Everything that's good for you can also be bad for you. It depends on who the I is and how you go about doin' what you do. I an' I been usin' weed for years upon years now and it never made I eat out of garbage even once. On the other hand I know of brothers who after only two shots them start whisperin' secrets to the moon at night. In the same way some brothers just never touch the thing at all. Playin' it safe. They don't believe in takin' chances—you know? Goin' out on a limb for personal satisfaction."

"Well," Hector said, "I believe in takin' chance but not those kinds. And I think those guys are damn right too."

Sugar Cane took another whiff. "Some people are cowards, that's why they never get anywhere in life."

"With all your bravery, I can't see where you've reached."

"But, brother, I an' I still alive! *Time will tell,* words of the great Bob Marley."

Hector slapped at a mosquito on his arm, the sound echoed as if he were in a big empty room. *"You think you're in heaven but you livin' in hell!...*The rest of the line."

Sugar Cane smiled. "I see the I know a little 'bout the king."

"Well, his songs play so much on the radio you can't help but. Some of his songs really sound... alright though. But that doesn't mean he's not a fool just like the rest of you. Look at the way he died for Christ's sake. Amputate a part of you foot or die and you choose death! And at a time when things couldn't be better! Now if that's not foolish I don't know what is."

"The man died because of what he believed in, brother," Sugar Cane said defensively. "If more of us had the guts to even stand up for what we believe in, politicians and them capitalist friends wouldn't have us by the balls like them do now. We're too afraid of dyin' and seein' blood so we succumb to humiliation and ego deflation. I'm no advocate of violence, but if we cared any at all about the future of this country and our children who will live here, we would have given the politicians a clear message a long time ago. Another Paul Bogle would be welcome any day now."

Hector found himself nodding in total agreement to this. "Guess you have a point."

"I have more than a point, brother," Sugar Cane continued. "What I have is about ten gallon with more bubblin' over every day."

This was another thing Hector couldn't stand with these Rastas. They constantly changed the meaning of common words to suit their argument. Now, how the fuck he managed to substitute *pint* for *point* and still wanted people to believe the weed had not gone to his head was beyond Hector. Hector sighed and threw his eyes to the heavens but said nothing of it. Quite likely it would only get worse if he pointed it out to Sugar Cane.

"So," Hector said, "When's the woman comin' up?" He wanted to get the conversation on a smoother path.

"The who?"

"The woman... your wife, lady, chickeeta—whatever you guys call them."

"No brother, I don't live like that. I an' I is a African at heart, the one-woman thing can't hold me... I an' I want space to roam like a lion." Sugar Cane stopped to think and then added, "And besides, even if I ultimately decide to go into that sort of thing I'd have to have a house of I own first. It's bad enough that I have to be hop-scotchin' from rent house to rent house and I don't want to bring my queen and I children into that sort of situation. It just not healthy. No offence, brother, but I can't understand how you do it."

"No offence taken," Hector said and thought, *believe me, I wonderin' how I do it too... and why?*

"How long the I been livin' here?" Sugar Cane asked.

"'Bout four years," Hector told him.

"Lucky you. The longest I've ever stayed in a rented house before gettin' notice is eight months. From the moment the other tenants see I'm a rastaman they start for the landlord to evict me. It's like I have a disease they don't want to catch. ...But then, I an' I use to that sort of treatment from I own family, so strangers doin' it don't get me down too much."

"Your own family? So you're telling me you're the only Rasta in your family?"

Sugar Cane shook his head quickly. "Not really. I an' I old man was a Rasta too. It's because of him why I'm in it. Him use to be part of the Catholic church with the rest of I an' I relatives. But from early out he said he couldn't accept the white perception of God nor the fact that the Catholic church among others actually used the same Bible and teachings to enslave his forefathers. So he read the Bible for himself in his search for the truth. Rastafari was the truth that he found. Rent house people haven't found it yet though. I an' I can only pray for them." Sugar Cane paused to pull on the joint. "And the funny thing is I can't wait to see the day when I an' I never have to live in a rent house. I don't have much of a choice now for I don't have the sort of money these real estate people are askin'. Not even a quarter of it, for that matter. I an' I old man had a little house but when him pass on, him uncle and brothers and cousins just full it up. And because they weren't Rastas they just created all sorts of misery for I an' I till I just decided it was best to go try find some place of I own. Guess I made a mistake there. But as always, I an' I keepin the faith and hopin' that soon enough Selassie will shower me with his blessin's."

Hector got up, stretching till the joints in his back popped. He wasn't in the frame of mind to sit here listening to a rastaman's hard luck story. He had his own to worry about. "I think this is it for me," he said and turned to go inside.

"Sure," Sugar Cane said and made himself more comfortable in his seat. "I'll just stay here a little longer and soak up some of the fresh air."

"With all that smoke you're making it won't be fresh for much longer," Hector commented and went inside.

As he slipped into bed beside Sharon, he turned over in his mind all Ken and the beast had expressed. He guessed love was the reason he had decided to live with Sharon in the first place, but now he seriously questioned whether he loved her still. These days he felt as if what he had done was imprison himself, and now he wanted to break free. Only, after five years of having someone this close it just wasn't easy to do, almost as if you needed major surgery. *It's as easy as you make it,* ran in his mind again—but was this really true?

He glanced at the sleeping woman, her breaths short and deep. She didn't seem as beautiful as she had back at that career expo anymore. And the curves of her body had long ago ceased to arouse him. It was like sharing the bed with his mother.

Whenever he had sex with her these days, it was because it was just natural for people to get horny and when he did, she was available. There was no other reason in his mind, he simply wanted to release that caged up energy. That was all. Sometimes in the silence of the night, like now, he would think about all this, and it actually made him feel terrible to think that what he had thought was going to be a wonderful life with a beautiful woman had turned out to this.

87

Hector White sighed deeply and closed his eyes. As he fell off into a shallow sleep the thought foremost in his head was, *I want to roam like a lion too.*

CHAPTER EIGHT

SHARON AND the rastaman enjoyed each other's company more and more each day. They would meet by the ackee tree, mostly in the afternoons after she had come home from work. She didn't allow Hector to come home and see them there anymore, for she knew how he was. And if she didn't remember that it was time to get up and go warm Hector's dinner, Sugar Cane would remind her—for he knew how Hector was, too. Inevitably, there were times when Hector got home a little earlier than usual and would see them there chatting and laughing or singing some song. At these times, he would walk past them as usual and go inside, and Sharon would get up and follow him with the urgency of Cinderella at midnight to get his dinner ready. Sugar Cane would throw his head back and laugh at her.

What did they talk about? Anything at all, really. It was the mere fact that they were spending time together that delighted them. And secretly each knew that it delighted them more than either of them would want to express openly. For Sharon, it was the feeling of being appreciated that wooed her the most. Sugar Cane seemed to genuinely enjoy the conversations and found her jokes funny. It had been a while since anyone in this yard made her feel like that. Before he came along, this place was one of her main sources of unease. Which was very bad, since this place was her home. But that had changed now. Home was once again the place she wanted to rush back to from anywhere else. Of course, there was also a physical attraction to the roots man, but she actively tried to ignore this, for things could turn out pretty complicated if she didn't.

Though he didn't make it obvious, Sugar Cane was the weaker when it came to denying the chemistry between them. Even as they spoke of music and politics he couldn't help mentally drooling all over her body. Especially, when she moved her legs in such a way that her skirt shifted, revealing just a fraction of her thighs or she wore a blouse that hugged her breasts and pronounced her cleavage. He had to pray hard every night because of this; and he also had to masturbate every night because of this.

Guitar lessons were introduced when they honestly had nothing to talk about. Barring this, it wasn't even brought up. Sharon wasn't catching on as well as she had hoped, and she was gradually realising that she would love to play but didn't have the patience to learn. Sugar Cane was always ready to teach her, though, for it gave him the chance to get closer to her without seeming objectionable. Despite his burning desires, however, he had enough self control to start tutoring only when she told him she was ready to learn.

Whenever Sharon went to the market these weekends, all Ruby and Grace wanted to hear about was this new friend she'd found. It was like a main event. The first time she ever mentioned that there was this rastaman living at the house, the first thing Ruby asked, from behind her yam pile, was, "So what the gentleman name?"

"Joseph McCoy," Sharon told her, "But everybody calls him Sugar Cane."

"What a piece a bashment," Grace commented with a laugh that bubbled from her tubby body. "Is how him have such a sweet name?"

"He said that when he was a child he enjoyed eating sugar canes and left school early sometimes so he could visit the cane fields before he went by the record studio," Sharon said. "So his friends stuck the name on him. But he is really sweet though."

"Nuh so the whole a dem stay at the start?" the wiry Ruby asked. "Just the bes' thing dat can happ'n to you at first? Den them become you worse nightmare, embarrassin' you an' beatin' up on you if you question them foolish behaviour." Ruby had very black skin and teeth that used to be a comparable white but were now distant yellow due to years of neglect and constant smoking. For a forty-two year old woman who had borne two children, her stomach was rather flat, blending in well with her lanky build.

"I might be wrong," Sharon said, "but I don't think he's like that at all."

"So wha' 'bout Hector?" Grace asked. "How him feelin' 'bout dis rastaman?"

"Well he doesn't like the fact that he's there. But I think he hates it more because I don't seem to mind." She paused, reflecting for a while before adding, "But I don't care!... Well, I do, but I can't let his stupid attitude prevent me from having a good friend.

And besides, Hector isn't treating me good anyway."

"Damn right, girl!" Ruby agreed. "What him expect you to do? Sit around like a piece of furniture? You is a woman with feelin's, jus' like him is a man. Him want to go out everyday an' meet new people an' you should stay home an' be a good girl. None of that! Them days deh done, you nuh tell Hector? You need people to talk to too, an' if him not talkin' to you then—by God!—him shouldn't be saying anythin' 'bout you findin' some-one else who will. Them day dead an' you should make him know that shit!" Ruby always got like this when Hector was brought up in their conversations, for Sharon had given them the run-down of just how bad things were back at home. "Anyway though, Miss Sharon," Ruby then said with a mischievous smile curled on her thin lips, "make we stop makin' this man spoil our time together. Let's talk 'bout you new-found friend. The bashment man. You think you goin' ever give him some of yuh ackee?" The question came with a giggle. And before Sharon could reply, Ruby called to a woman shopper passing by, apparently looking around for a bargain on yams, "Ten dolla' a pound for the nice yam, lady." The lady, weighted by the black, plastic bag of goods she had on one arm, looked a little longer then walked on. Soon she was lost in the stream of buyers which, from an overhead view, would probably resemble an army of confused ants.

"What ackee?" Sharon asked with mocked ignorance.

"She nuh understan', Ruby tell har another way," Grace said. She was slicing off a piece of yam to be weighed and sold to the young woman who now stood in front of her. The woman wore a black leather suit and Grace couldn't help but wonder just how uncomfortable she must be feeling under this sweltering Saturday afternoon sun. The things young people did to make a statement, she thought.

"Alright," Ruby said. "You plan to take any yam from him? Him might have big, sweet yam you know!"

Sharon blushed. "Mind! People might hear you," she said.

"Oh come now, Miss Sharon," Ruby went. "Everybody too busy with them own thing to listen to us talkin' 'bout yam an' ackee. An' if somebody even hear, it nuh make nuh difference. Them nuh have a clue what we talkin' 'bout."

Ruby was right, Sharon thought. This was the place you could shout your secrets and they remained just secrets. The place was just too full of different conversations at any one time for anyone passing by to give concentrated attention to a particular one. It was like a bargaining pit at a trade center. And besides, the code names, yam and ackee, were foolproof. Sharon still didn't answer, however—couldn't, really. The mere fact that she knew what Ruby was talking about was inhibiting her speech.

"Silence mean consent," Grace said and they all found it quite funny.

"After all," Ruby went on in support of Grace's point, "you usual yam supplier not givin' enough anymore so you must want to take at least a little bit from another farmer. The new one may even be better than you ever tasted. You just never know."

"You never know," Grace echoed, "Him might just have the goodly pum-pum yam!"

Ruby said, "Him will want the ackee though. Even if you don't want the yam, him will want the ackee. Man is like that; them love ackee, an' though them don't always say them want it, if them gettin' it them not refusin' it. If them ever refuse it, is because them want to be faithful to them wife, is not because them don't want it. Man is like that."

"That's so true," Grace agreed.

Sharon said nothing. She smiled and kept an impassive countenance that revealed just as little as she said.

***

"And who is this Sugar Cane, dear," Ronald Gordon asked when she called to wish them merry Christmas. It wasn't her intention to mention the name but it just sort of slipped out in her conversation as she related just how she had been keeping these days. Anyway, it didn't matter if her father did know of Sugar Cane for he really couldn't choose her friends for her now could he?

"He's a friend, Daddy," she told him. "He lives in the back room of the house. He's a Rastafarian."

"I see," Ronald said and then directed his voice to Margaret who was instructing the helper just how to arrange the drapes, "You hear that, dear? Your daughter now has some new friend named Sugar Cane. Says he's a Rastafarian."

"I know that," Margaret returned, "she told me all about him when we last spoke."

Ronald grunted. "Apparently I'm the only one constantly left in the dark."

"Apparently," Margaret said. "Ask her to say hi to him for me."

Ronald ignored the request. "So, how's Hector?"

It was only then Sharon realised she had not mentioned Hector's name even once. "He's fine," she told her father as she thought, *next thing I tell you things aren't going so well and you start with that I-told-you-so thing again.* "Hector's just fine."

"Will you be coming to spend Christmas with us, Sharon?" Ronald asked. "It's been a while you know."

Sharon sighed. *It has been a while,* she thought, but still she didn't think this year was the time to make a trip to England. She couldn't say why for sure, but she didn't think she was willing to leave Sugar Cane for that long. *Not yet.* Maybe it was because the friendship was only just growing. She should be taking about three weeks leave in January, maybe she could go visit them then. She had long ago promised Ruby she would be spending most of that time at her place but she could always cut that visit short to go to England for a while. "Maybe in January," she told Ronald. But somewhere inside she felt she wouldn't be making it then either.

***

Sharon invited Sugar Cane to church on Christmas morning but he turned her down. However, on New Year's Eve they struck a deal; he would go to church with her if she went to the Nyabingi Temple with him the following week. She agreed. He had a lot to criticise about pastor Granstan's attitude and the whole conduct of the service especially when the pastor said, "Some of you thinkin' that dog is God, pot is God and Selassie is God—but I tell you if you don't get Jesus in you souls you goin' fart!" On the other hand, she totally enjoyed the Nyabingi meeting a week later. She even bought herself a Rastafarian bracelet on her way home. Of course Hector couldn't know this, so she kept it hidden and wore it only when she was at the clinic.

CHAPTER NINE

LET JAH LEAD
By Sugar Cane

CHORUS:
Let Jah lead, let Jah lead.
Just give him the chance
And he'll fulfill your needs.
Forget the want and the greed,
Let him lead, let him lead,
Let Jah lead, let Jah lead.

VERSE 1:
When you have those problems all around you
And all you think about is giving up,
There's always something else you can do-ooo!
Something that can make your problems stop.

CHORUS

VERSE 2:
He will never let you feel alone,
As long as you ask for his company,
You don't have to use the telephone, no-ooo!
Just open up your heart and make your plea.

CHORUS

CHAPTER TEN

SUGAR CANE had his next appointment with Touch in the second week of 1997. By this another well of confidence had started in him. It was a new year and that meant your luck could change any day. Unfortunately, his didn't. *Let Jah Lead* was flatly refused. "Try the church," Touch suggested with an annoyed giggle. "All they'll have to do is probably change the Jah to Jesus and you gone clear fi Sunday morning, dreadlocks."

Naturally, all this didn't add to Sugar Cane's confidence as a song writer. Many questions crowded his mind. A prominent one was, why was he doing this to himself? Why did he not just follow everybody else's advice and go all out for the money? Write what will sell! Don't be such an ass! For if he wasn't in the business for the money, what the hell was he in it for then?

Artistic fulfullment? a voice suggested.

Give me a break, said another.

It wasn't the artistic fulfillment—at least not exclusively. He got most of that just doing one-night gigs at hotels and night clubs. This was what paid the bills, which meant it was sometimes treated as just another job, but it also gave him much fulfillment. He was never really the best voice on this or any other side of town but he could sing—and when he did people rocked and cheered. This was artistic fulfillment and it wasn't what he longed for.

What is it then, dreadlocks? Destiny? His mind shouted at him. No, it wasn't just his mind. It was Touch's voice full of mockery and ridicule. *What the fuck is it?*

Sugar Cane really couldn't answer—at least not now.

When he got home he sat on the bed and cried. It was the first he could remember crying since his father's passing and in a way he was surprised at himself. Not that he thought he was out of tears, but he never thought the constant rejections of his songs would ever bring him to this state. Sugar Cane always believed that each rejection meant that he should work harder at making the next attempt better. So, strangely, they had always acted as a sort of motivation. But now he wasn't so sure what they represented—or meant.

Warm tears bled from the creases of his fingers as he brought his palms to mask his face. He was thirty years old. Where was his life going? What was he really doing? Had he been fooling himself all along? Was he really ever going to make it as a song writer? Maybe he should have gone on to college, he thought. Maybe he should have resisted the urge to press on with the dream, no matter what. *How... How did I bring myself to believin' that? No matter what? Sink or swim?*

The questions came at him like fire darts and Selassie just wasn't showing him the answers. Inside he was genuinely lost, uncertain.

In time the tears abated. Now all that remained were sniffles and vampire-red eyes. Stretching himself out across the bed he reached for the Bible he had placed under his pillow after praying last night. His hands trembled when he touched its cool, leather binding. Just then he heard the knock at the door. He replaced the holy book and went to see who it was.

It was Sharon, a white Pyrex dish held carefully with both hands. She still had on her apron and a plaid dish towel slung over the shoulder.

"I think you've been here long enough for you to know what my cooking tastes like. Are you curious?" She smiled as she spoke, handing over the container to him like it were the key to the city. *Maybe it was.* "Actually, I thought you'd be too tired when you got home to do any cooking yourself."

He took it firmly in his hand. "Thanks," he told her lifting the lid. The warm aroma of steamed fish and rice unearthed his appetite. Her thoughtfulness touched him to the point where he was grabbing at his mind for something to say. He had told her he was going to knock at every producer's door today but he never said it with any intention of evoking such a deed. "You didn't have to do this," was the best he could do.

"I know," she said.

Again he was left speechless. Her gesture meant more to him than she probably realised, for it told him that she thought of him even while he was out of her sight.

"Come inside," he said. "Have a seat for a while." He gestured somewhat self-consciously, to the single chair he had in the room by his desk. "I promise you won't turn to stone." Sugar Cane smiled.

Sharon hesitated, then came inside for she couldn't find an excuse not to. It was the time of day they'd normally spend by the ackee tree. But this was the first she had ever seen what inside his room looked like. Red, green and yellow everywhere. The curtains, a copy of the Ethiopian flag. Selassie's distinguished face hung in frames on every wall, a constant reminder, Sharon thought, if Sugar Cane ever needed one of what his God looked like. She looked around in sheer awe and much interest.

Sugar Cane, on the other hand, saw it all everyday so there was nothing to distract him from putting the lid of the dish aside and digging into the food as soon as his fingers got hold of a fork from the dish drainer. It really tasted better than anything he could have whipped up for himself at any time. As Sharon watched him eat, it reminded her of last Christmas when she had taken some dinner to Mrs. Bailey's. When her grandson came into the room and saw the food on the table he was pleasantly surprised. Not that he hadn't eaten, but more food was always good news. What Sharon remembered most about this though was how he took up the dish and, seeing that some had already been taken out by his grandmother, asked, "So wha' you say Granny, me can work dis?"

"If you caa' work it?" Mrs. Bailey had asked. She had a goat's voice. "What you mean by that, Lipton?"

"Me mean if me caa' eat it, Granny," Lipton replied.

"Me wi' neva understan' dem yah young people way a talkin' at all, at all," Mrs. Bailey had said. Yet sometime later when she actually got up and went out to the porch where she saw Lipton scooping the food into his mouth she had to say, "Lipton you caan' tek time? Now a know wha' you mean when you say you a work the food! You jus' a nyam it so lack a hog!"

Right now Sharon had to admit that Sugar Cane too was really *working* the food.

"You really believe he's God, don't you?" she asked, sitting in the chair.

Sugar Cane glanced up from the dish. He saw her eyes were glued to the man on the wall. "Up until recently, yes, but right now I an' I not so sure what to say." His speech was muffled as his mouth was engorged with fish and rice.

"Was it that bad?" she asked, turning her attention to him now. He had told her his plans yesterday so she knew all about it and its importance to him. More and more she was knowing about his plans for each day, more than she had ever been privileged to know about Hector's. In a similar fashion, Sugar Cane listened to all her shared thoughts, throwing in a suggestion or two when necessary. They both liked doing this very much. It gave them the opportunity to express themselves in a way conducive to good platonic relationships.

"Worse... I just don't know what to think right now. It's always advisable to be strong and keep the faith, but I an' I can't help but wonderin' sometimes, if this string of low blows will ever end in my lifetime. I an' I also ask myself why was Selassie doin' this to me when I try my best to serve him? Of course, you don't have to ask where my thoughts go from there?" He chowed down some more food.

"Maybe he's testing your faith—you know, like Job in the Bible? Maybe it's goin' to end any day now... Maybe–"

"Maybe not! It's just one fuckin' nightmare, that's what it is."

She was stunned by his language. From Hector, yes, but not from Sugar Cane. And he didn't apologise, which meant it didn't come out by accident. It sounded exotic coming out of his mouth. And in a way Sharon admired that very human part of him.

They didn't speak for a while after this, but the silence was far from boring or uncomfortably heavy. Instead, it was more like another sort of way to communicate feelings. The mere fact that she simply sat there through it all was a message in itself, too. It told Sugar Cane that she didn't mind just being with him if only for his quiet company.

Sugar Cane ate everything, chewing bones and swallowing whatever parts of them he could. Despite his woes, Sharon thought, he still managed to have an appetite. *Or maybe it's just the unrelenting hunger talking, Sharon. Maybe he has been so anxious about getting the song ready for the producer's ear he simply didn't have the time to eat much. If you notice all his pots and pans are all clean and dry in the dish drainer. When was this all done? Last night or three days ago?* Sugar Cane licked his fingers like a child. This brought a smile to her face. *Probably three days ago.*

"See," he said when he was done, "you waited a while and you didn't turn to stone." Sugar Cane put the dish on the table at the far end of the room and covered it over with a towel so the flies didn't have anything to play crows with.

"Sister, it seems like you is the only one who thinks about I an' I. What do I say?" He leaned forward, stroking her cheek with the back of his hand. Sharon could feel her face going flush and her spine tingling. And when he tentatively pulled his hand away, her cheek followed like steel to a powerful magnet. This was what she longed for.

103

Then she realised what was actually happening. Instantly, she stood up and hurried over to one of Selassie's pictures on the wall. Sharon stared at it with intense interest but wasn't actually seeing it. There were other things on her mind. *Leave,* she told herself, *take the things and leave. You're both alone and the door is closed. Hector won't be home for another half hour at least. Anything can happen. Anything!*

But Sharon Marva Gordon wasn't ready to leave. Not yet. The sweetness of just knowing she was behind closed doors with this man was overwhelming. She was scared, too, but not enough to want to walk out the door and never return. Not enough to ignore the sweetness.

Her back was still turned to him when she asked, "Where is your woman?"

Sugar Cane sighed. "My woman."

Sharon could hear him shifting uncomfortably. "Thought I'd never ask?" She sensed his unease and started feeling the same. Actually, she had been afraid to ask, afraid of what the answer might be. He had never raised the topic either, which made her fear even greater. The most persistent questions were, *is he married and doesn't want to tell me? Is his wife somewhere right at this moment wondering how to locate her man?* But now she just had to know—no matter how it made her feel.

"Thought I'd never have to talk about that."

She turned to face him. Apparently he wasn't married after all. At least, that was what she wanted to be the case. And even if he was married, it wasn't going so great. Secretly, she somehow felt good about this *if-I-can't-have-him-you-can't-have-him-either* syndrome. It was a very selfish way to think but it was also very human.

"Oh! You don't have to if you find it difficult... I was only trying to make conversation." She hoped he did want to continue, however. This, too, was very human.

He suddenly smiled at her. "Gatha did want more from life than I an' I was able to provide, so she left me for someone who could give her everythin' she want."

"I'm sorry."

"It's the real world. Sometimes you win but most times you lose. That's why winnin' seem so special."

"Did you love her?" She glided closer to him, this time sitting on the bed.

"Too much," he said reflectively. "That's why I try not to bring her up. Hurt like hell when I an' I think of how stupid I was to think that she was goin' to stick around when all she ever did was mope about the hairstyles she couldn't afford and the clothes she'd love to wear."

It came to his memory all too clearly. The way he and Gatha lived together for two years and three rented apartments, planning for a future together and all that shit. "What would I ever do without you?" she used to ask him in the wee hours of the morning after what she called one of his satisfying screws.

The answer had come to her when she visited Touch's studio one night and met Max. He called himself The Max, a smooth-talking, cloud-walking fart who thought he was the best singer in the world. Quite a few people seemed to think so too, for they bought his music no matter how dumb the lyrics sounded. *"The*

Max man's gonna riip you away from you man an' proviide you with the sort a liiife-a-livin' you truly deserve," were his words the very moment the 'cool-dude' turned and saw Gatha enter the studio holding Sugar Cane's hand. Even now Sugar Cane could not forget that line. At the time it didn't mean much, for Gatha really hadn't seemed impressed by it—but that very line turned out to be prophecy.

In no more than three weeks of secret rendevous and a special delivery of red roses, Gatha was hooked and by the end of that month she was gone. Sugar Cane had come home one day to see the goodbye note on the same bed they'd made love in the night before. *The goodbye screw,* he now thought. He could have gone hunting after her for he knew where The Max had his cool-dude pad but he decided not to. If you gave your all to a woman, he thought, and she still wanted to go, let her. Not letting her go would quite likely have made his life more hellish than the hurt her absence could induce.

"I'm learnin' to move on, though," he said to Sharon with an air of finality. And then, as an afterthought, he added with a melancholy smile, "Who wants a woman name Gatha, anyway?"

Sharon kissed him on his cheek. She did it because she found it the best way to tell him she genuinely felt his pain. But she also did it because desire drove her to—in the same way you'd probably be tempted to going way over the speed limit on a straight road that was well paved and clear for as far as your eyes could see.

Sugar Cane had the same feeling of desire, too. Only his temptation lead him to pulling her even closer and guiding his lips to hers. She was reluctant. "Just a single kiss," he touted. "Just–"

–One, Sharon told herself but then she turned away again. She got up. "I must go now." She got the Pyrex and started for the door. She fought hard to suppress the fire which raged inside her because Hector wasn't doing what he was supposed to be doing. The fire which was making her almost unable to think clearly about the consequences.

"Sharon, wait!" Sugar Cane called. She stopped. He stood up, but didn't try to get closer as he feared that would only scare her away. It was like trying to catch a wild dove, patience was necessary. "Please stay."

Bracing against her emotions, Sharon opened the door and left. Her feet felt like heavy metal cast in cement but she managed to lift them and hurry away.

A first thought told him to go after her even if he had to go to her bedroom to get that kiss, but he quickly figured that would be foolish. So he watched her go, the bundle in his pants painfully hard. He thought she was just as hard-up in her own feminine way.

He closed the door then threw himself across the bed, his locks splashing out about him. Here he would remain till the feeling was gone. Exodus 20 verse 17 ran into his mind again and for a while he was taken aback by it. *This must be the only time Selassie think him should intervene,* he thought and smiled. *Well, at least it shows me you're still around.*

"Thou shalt not covet thy neighbour's wife," he said in a sighing whisper. "Guess I'll have to make her mine, then. That way I won't have to covet I an' I neighbour anymore."

107

CHAPTER ELEVEN

HECTOR DIDN'T realise what was happening. Either that or he just didn't give a fuck. The signs were now too clear that Sharon didn't think much of the way he treated her anymore. No matter how late he came in, she didn't question it or complain like she used to; and if he never said a word to her all day she didn't seem to mind much. Sharon had other things on her mind. She had Sugar Cane on her mind. She spoke of the rastaman in Hector's presence almost every day. She would speak of his songs and just how she believed he was going to shock the world one day when it finally got a chance to hear his music. Of his philosophical views of blacks, Rastafarianism, Christianity and how they all fitted into the big picture. Of marginalisation of the black male, repatriation of the mind, and ozone depletion.

"Every day Sugar Cane this, Sugar Cane that! You don't have anythin' better to talk 'bout? That rastaman just fullin' up you head with all sorts of unnecessary shit! He'll soon start sayin' he's God and I bet you you'll believe that, too." This was all he had ever said on the matter.

But how she wished he would say more! Maybe warn her

against allowing Sugar Cane to come between them. Tell her that things weren't the best now but someday soon it would change and he would find a way—some way!—to love her again like he used to. Mention the word *need* a time or two. Hold her some-times—even if he didn't really feel like it. Hold her anyway because he wanted things to work out and there was still hope. Hope like the hope that Sugar Cane held on to. Hope that said no matter how dismal things may seem they *were* going to get better. Then maybe—and a very probable maybe, too—that would get her thinking of what they had to lose.

The girls at the market were all for what was happening. They always wanted to hear the new developments and Sharon always wanted to tell.

"You know it comin' any day now?" Ruby asked when Sharon told them of what had almost happened behind Sugar Cane's closed doors. "Any day now you goin' to get that lovely piece a yam you been hopin' for so long."

"Ruby, stop it," Sharon said, "I haven't been hoping for any-thing."

"That's wha' you keep tellin' us, but we know betta—eeeh, Grace?" Ruby weighed a pound of yellow yam—the pum-pum type—and handed it to a customer. She collected $10.

"She tryin' to deny it," Grace said with a teasing snicker.

She was denying it from them, but to her nothing was more true. It had been a week and a day now since she almost allowed herself to give in to her feelings, and ever since then she had simply kept out of Sugar Cane's sight. Once she was home, Sharon didn't come outside—especially in the afternoons when she knew Sugar Cane would be coming out to the ackee tree to practice his songs. *But for how long are you not going to see him?* Not much longer, she knew, for each day she stayed away she could literally feel her heart fluttering for dear life. This had never happened to her before. And each day it got worse. So, soon, she knew, she would have to see him again—no matter how afraid she was of what might happen when she did.

But why be afraid? It's not like Hector mattered anymore, she thought. But it wasn't Hector now and she knew it. It was the relationship! No matter how bad it was going, the fact was she was in one and her own principles made for it difficult for her to break the rules.

"Let har deny it all she want," Ruby said. "Mi jus' hope that Sugar Cane have enough yam to eat with all that ackee she must have savin' up by this."

"And to think," Grace added, "ackee is in full season now."

Ruby grunted. "That only make it worse!"

CHAPTER TWELVE

SUGAR CANE came in and pushed the door behind him. He was just coming from the river where he'd had an invigorating bath and swim. There was no water in the pipes today but on several other occasions over the past months he found himself going there even when there was water around. It was simply that pleasurable, the cold water beating down on his locks from the falls and the smell of nature all around him.

He took off all his clothes and began drying himself more thoroughly with a big red beach towel he took from his dresser drawer. The fact that he was now naked and the door had not gone shut when he'd pushed it, didn't bother him for he wasn't prudish where this was concerned. And besides, he had too much on his mind to be worried about closing the door while he dried himself.

He had Sharon on his mind.

It was three days over a solid week now since they last met face to face. He knew, for he was counting. She had kept away from him and he had kept away from her, too. Things were moving a little too fast for him, and he—just like Sharon—was afraid. Afraid he might just get involved before the time was right. But when was the time right? When she became his and not Hector's.

When he didn't have to covet his neighbour's wife.

He took the bottle of olive oil from the dresser. He had performed at Jah-Jah Son's restaurant last night and his muscles now ached. It had been a good performance and he was thankful for the five thousand dollars it brought him. If it was one thing about Jah-Jah Son, he had never forgotten an old friend in need, Sugar Cane thought.

"Have a job for you," were Jah-Jah Son's first words as Sugar Cane opened the door to his knocks last night. He was smiling and Sugar Cane could notice that he was now sporting gold teeth where the empty spaces had been.

"A *job*?" Sugar Cane had asked after duly greeting his friend and ushering him inside. As he spoke Sugar Cane prepared two glasses of Irish moss.

"Yes, I," Jah-Jah Son said. "It's like the business gettin' a little better. Maybe is the food an' maybe is my cute face–" he smiled and nodded, "–but the customers jus' findin' it the place to be when them jus' want a place to chill out. Jus' like I an' I plan it. So I man decide to... *capitalize* on this by givin' them some live music three nights a week. Naturally, as a long-time brethren, you is the first person I think of. An' you can sing, too."

"Give thanks, give thanks," Sugar Cane had said. It now meant that he could expect to get some money on a weekly basis, as long as customers kept on coming to Jah-Jah Son's restaurant.

He was going to do his part to make sure this was indeed the case.

Sugar Cane poured just a touch of the oil in his palm. This he used to massage his shoulders. It felt real good but he couldn't help but wishing it was Sharon's hands that did it instead of his own.

Just after ten, he saw from the wrist watch which rested on the dresser. Soon the sun would be so hot you couldn't believe last night coming into this morning had been pleasantly cool. Like always, he would soon go hacking at the songs. There were times when he thought it would be good to just forget about song writing and get on with whatever was left of his life—but that was easier said than done. The last rejection had shaken him up so badly that he had told himself, he wouldn't be writing any more songs for a while. Only, the next morning there he was—as usual—with his guitar, pencil and legal pad, and was halfway through a new song before realising he had already broken his resolution. Just like Jah-Jah Son had told him.

Time for the back, he thought, turning that part of his body to the mirror. And just as he began to hook his arm to get as far up on his back as possible, the door flew wide open.

CHAPTER THIRTEEN

IT WAS that same morning that Sharon's anxiety got the better of her. Her leave had just started, giving her all the time in the world to think about what was happening between herself and Sugar Cane. This thing had gone on for too long now, she thought, and she just had to see him—even if for some reason he didn't want to see her. To be on the safe side, though, she would wait till he was by the ackee tree to do it. She wouldn't go to his room like she had the last time they spoke, for she knew very well what could happen.

After seeing Hector off to work, she found yesterday's copy of the Gleaner and stretched out on the bed to read it. But the words on the paper meant nothing to her. The bold headlines made some sense, but the little black words seemed out of mental focus. Her mind just wasn't prepared to deal with anything more than the matter at hand.

And, she thought, was there ever a time when Hector had this effect on her? Maybe—but she couldn't remember. He had been sweet and caring and all that, but she couldn't remember herself not being able to eat or sleep because she was missing him. This only brought her to wonder, had she ever really loved Hector? Or did she merely decide to be his girl because she was fond of him and *he* really loved her? But was she still fond of him now? And did he still really love her? What was the line in that Whitney Houston song? *If somebody loves you, won't they always love you?... Always!* Maybe not, Sharon thought, maybe not at all.

She folded the paper and tossed it aside. She couldn't wait till later. She just had to see him now! Her heart galloped excitedly in her chest as she swung her legs to the floor and got up, moving as fast as she could. In less than a minute she was out her door and headed for his. She still had no idea of what she was first going to say to him, but that didn't matter. Something would come out.

The door was ajar, she saw as she came to it and stopped. Through the long crack, she could just see his back. It was fascinatingly firm and almost as dark as coffee. He seemed to be admiring himself in the mirror. Sharon couldn't help but feeling like an intruder and for a split second thought of turning back to return later. But she knew she couldn't do that—*not now!* To think of retreating was not even a remote possibility.

So for a while she stood there, watching him rub some sort of lotion over his shoulders; and she thought, *I should be the one doing that for you.* She could smell the freshness of the soap he had used to bathe this morning.

He has a really cute butt, she thought slyly. And she admired the way his locks just rested on the brink of it, too. The black of his hair standing out like steel filings on magnet against his skin. He seemed impressively powerful from where she stood—as if he could handle any situation this world had to offer. Yes, Sharon Gordon was lusting.

Was this what it had been all along? Lust? Sharon didn't think so. Her heart told her there was more to it than that. And as far as she knew, only the heart could truly tell the difference between love and lust. Right now though, it was the lust for the man, not the love, that stood out. Like the last time, she was feeling rather hot, as if she wanted to get out of the polka-dot cotton dress she had on. Take it off and let him see–

Sharon was breathing so heavily now she worried that he might hear her. But he seemed to be so taken up with himself he wouldn't be hearing anything. Nervously she looked around to make sure there was no one watching her, then went back to peeking.

Sharon go home, a voice told her. *How could you be doing this to Hector? How could you? End the RELATIONSHIP first, then you can do whatever you want. But until then it's just so... wrong. Women like you don't do these things to your men. You should be strong—no matter what!*

Guilt set in again and this time she felt like she really should be going. Just one last look, she thought, just one.

It was at this point that Sugar Cane turned round to get his backside facing the mirror. The frontal view, she saw, was even more impressive. So much so that it made her gape and stumble forward. She tried desperately to regain her balance, but failed. She tumbled into his arms, uttering a mute shriek as she felt them hold her. Throughout this scene her eyes were shut tight as if wishing it away. The truth was, however, reality didn't just go away like that. It lingered—and you just had to find a way to deal with it.

When she did open her eyes, his were waiting. "I hope you're not sorry," he said.

She glanced back at the view of the yard that the open door gave her, then glanced back at him. "I was just coming to see you... It's been so long..."

"A week and three days," he agreed. "Why we let that happen?"

"I don't know." She shook her head slowly, still in a daze. "Does it matter?" She could feel his cock hardening against her. It felt good to be appreciated in this way.

"I guess not."

She was becoming an animal. She could feel it boiling up inside her like a wild cat fighting to be let loose. Like Grace said, ackee was in full season now. Yam seemed to be in season, too.

Sugar Cane guided Sharon's hand to his cock. It was as weighty as it looked. "It's huge." She smiled. *Animal.*

"Close the door," he told her. This she did with one hand, the other still holding the hard, throbbing cylinder.

In another five seconds Sharon Marva Gordon was naked, too.

CHAPTER FOURTEEN

HE ENTERED her from the back first. They were still standing, only now she was leaning forward against one of the walls, digging her fingers into the plaster work as he sent his cock whispering erotic secrets all the way up her cunt. She was hot and extremely tight when he had just begun penetrating. Then the heat blossomed into a lubricating wetness and the tightness assumed the form of a delightful suction that pulled his manliness upwards, deeper, deeper. Had he been as inexperienced as he was, say, ten years ago, he probably would have come all over her within mere seconds of this wonderful experience. And quite likely she would have used all this pent-up energy she was now using to spider-climb her way up the wall as his cock sank deeper still, to kill him. *Thank Selassie for him small mercies,* he thought, he was a man now and knew just how to rock the–

(the only thing in this life that all it hype up to be is pussy!)

–boat without sinking it. So he held her with strong arms and while touching her back and neck all over, slowly rotated the throbbing glans penis against the roof of her cunt.

Sharon squirmed and shuddered, digging her low-cut nails harder into the wall. One flushed cheek pressed up against Selassie's imperial face. Probably if Sugar Cane was seeing—or realising—this was happening, he would have changed the position, but at this moment he was far too focused to even remember who his God was. He was actually grunting like a wild boar as Sharon braced her ass and see-sawed his cock.

"Fuck it", she panted, reaching for his hand and guiding it to her breast. She then coaxed his firm fingers into gently kneading them like a dough. While he did this she fondled the triangle of red hair on her sweet cup. It all felt so very wonderful, it felt marvelous, it felt... "Oh yeees! Yeees! YEEES!" This was what she had been denying herself for so very long now. *This!*

Fuck it!

In a while they were down on the floor, Sugar Cane flat on his back and Sharon on top, bouncing on his cock like a jockey on a trotting stallion. Just beside them was the polka-dot dress she had taken off with such urgency it had ripped under one arm and at the waist. The black panties were somewhere in a corner where her impatient flick of the wrist had thrown it. Later they would both go on the hunt for it, but right now it just didn't matter.

It was the missionary position that ended it. Somehow, they had made it to the bed, both sweating and panting heavily. She held onto his locks as they both worked methodically to the point where he melted into her in a big gush. As he did this, she kissed him, full and deep, and whispered, "You understand me." They hugged each other and slept.

CHAPTER FIFTEEN

"WHAT ARE we going to do?" Sharon asked, her head resting on Sugar Cane's bare chest. They were both exhausted from hours of uncompromising sex. She couldn't remember the last time she had made herself so totally available to a man's untamed desires. It was as if she had never really made love until today. She could still feel the ghost of him inside her. It felt wonderful, yet it made her uneasy. The wrong that felt right. "This can't go on," she continued. She could hear his heartbeat.

"Can we pretend it never happen?" He spoke in a husky whisper, full of thought.

It didn't take her long to think this out. "No," she said.

"Then it has to go on then," he concluded, folding his arms to pillow his head, eyes concentrating on the watermarks on the ceiling.

"But what about your religion?"

His torso rolled up and down like an ocean wave as he sighed. "Selassie's been failin' I an' I for so long now, what could be so wrong with I an' I returnin' the favour once?"

"You don't mean that."

"I don't really. But what can I do? It's not like I can just wish these feelin's be gone and them obey!'

"We could try stay–"

"–Stayin' away from each other? Don't tell me you already forget how very well that went."

She could sense annoyance. Before today he had always been so patient with her but now that–

(he had gotten what he wanted?)

–they were more intimate, his tolerance level seemed to have dropped. She hoped this wasn't true. That he was like this because of the present situation. "I'm sorry," she said, running her fingers over his chest.

"I'm sorry, too. I didn't mean it to come out like that. It's just that this is so damn confusin'."

"If Hector finds out, it's going to be more than that."

He grunted. "Don't I know it. I an' I might end up havin' to kill him ass."

"What???" She rose up, startled.

"Gotcha!" he said and they both found a moment to laugh at the drama such a situation would have evoked.

"I got a job last night," he told her when the laughing had simmered down to gleaming smiles. "Three nights a week as long as business stay good."

"Really? That's wonderful!" she said.

He went on to giving her the details of how he got the job,

where exactly this Jah-Jah Son's restaurant was and how much he was expected to make each week. This explained to her why he rose so late this morning. Secretly, she had been thinking he had been out with some woman or the other. Maybe even Gatha! This world was a funny place where love could often- times make you the featured comedian.

They kissed till his hardness revitalised. Then they really made love—the sort you would associate with a rug by the fireplace, Johnny Mathis on the stereo, and an empty champagne bottle.

For the rest of the time no mention was made of Hector or Selassie. Whichever way possible, this simply had to go on.

Sharon didn't leave the rastaman's bed till it was time to go prepare Hector's dinner.

CHAPTER SIXTEEN

THE FEAST of ackee and yam had begun. Hardly a day passed now that Sharon and Sugar Cane didn't enjoy each other's body, once Hector was away. Naturally, they both had feelings of guilt, but that never stopped anything for passion always won out. There were also hurting bouts of jealousy as Sugar Cane was finding it very difficult to deal with Sharon's having to go home to Hector at all. Just knowing Hector was sleeping in the same bed with Sharon—probably even holding her as the nights grew older and cold—was devastating. It felt like Hector was intruding now: Sharon was his. He had earned her. And some nights, no matter how late he got home from Jah-Jah Son's, he just couldn't sleep because of this. The thought of Hector just accidentally dying, sometimes seemed quite viable.

Sharon was just as uneasy. She would feel dirty just knowing she had to be with Hector. At nights she would lay awake just watching him sleep, his mouth agape and his beer gut ballooning up and down as he snored and farted. The sight disgusted her. *Get up!* she would think. *Get up and go be with Sugar* (for this was all she called him now, *Sugar*). *Hector won't come awake till six. By then you'll be back inside preparing breakfast. He won't have a clue you'd been out.* Sharon didn't chance it through. Sometime in the night he might reach across and find her gone.

"Sharon, I can't stand this anymore," Sugar Cane told her one Tuesday afternoon as she got ready to leave him. "Let's tell him about us... Leave him!"

"I can't," she said. "Not yet; he'd kill me."

"I'd kill him first." Sugar Cane was serious.

"Don't talk like that. It scares me." She paused, then added, "I'll handle it, just give me some time, okay?"

Reluctantly he agreed. "Just don't take too long."

"I won't."

She didn't know the first move. What she did know, however, was that it was not the easiest thing to just get up and walk out of a five-year-old relationship—no matter how rocky it had become. It required much deliberation. Would a relationship with Sugar turn out like the one she was now in? It seemed all so wonderfully promising now, but she knew too well that this could all change. It could even get worse than the one she now had. For instance, Hector had never hit her. And Sugar had mentioned the word kill so many times in the past few days she could only wonder about the extent of this wrath. It took a lot of pushing to get him to the limit but when he did get there, what was he capable of doing?

Stick with the evil you know, Sharon. Hector frowns at you everyday now but there was a time when he used to smile. And who knows? He might just smile again.

Yeah, who knows?

And what were you telling Sugar about Hector killing you if you left him? Hector won't lay a finger on you and you know it. Well, he's never tried it before, but then I've never tried to leave him before either. People can get real weird when you mess around with their emotions. Some could take things pretty easy but others could get really fucking weird. I'll just have to be careful.

"Nuh put nothin' above him," was Ruby's remark when Sharon related her predicament to her. They were at Ruby's house as Sharon had kept her promise to spend some of her leave there. Truthfully, she didn't want to leave Sugar for an entire week, but—a promise was a promise—she had simply made her mind up to go through the motions. "Any man is capable of murder; that's what mi think—you just take you time an' let things work themself out."

'You really think so, Ruby?"

"Of course!" Ruby replied. "An' I don't think you should worry too much 'bout how things might finally turn out between you an' Sugar Cane. The fact is, you now feelin' better 'bout you'self than you felt in a long time. If for once in you life, girl, live for the moment!"

The topic faded as Ruby went to make lemonade for both of them. Sharon sat there in the living room, thinking about it all. She was feeling as if somewhere along the line, she had lost direction. At times like these, she even dared to think that her father may have been right all along: that she really didn't know what she wanted. She did.

Ruby brought the drinks and cookies to the table where they

sat and ate. It was just after noon, and Sharon had been here just about two hours now. Her bags were still packed and sitting on the bed in the room Ruby had prepared for her from the day before. William Smith was around the back, working on another set of baskets. Those he had made last week had all been sold by the second day. Since then he had simply been searching for the best material to start the next batch. Tommy and Christine should be coming home from school in another two and a half hours, and they would have their friends over, and the place would start sounding like a play pen. But right now it was quiet and peaceful.

"I just wish I could spend the nights with him, too," Sharon said to herself, her eyes dazed and full of fantasy.

Ruby heard her murmur. She sighed. "Then do it."

"How? You're the one who just agreed that I shouldn't try to go too fast."

A weary sigh escaped the other woman. "Well, maybe not *every* night that God send, but the few that you plan to spend here with me for instance, you could use otherwise. As long as, when you down there, you stay inside and don't come out for anybody to see you—Hector won't know a thing. Him will think you up here with me. It's not 'bout goin' too fast. It's 'bout knowin' how to work your way round the system, girl. An' believe mi, if you don't know how to work the system the system will surely work you."

Sharon glanced at the empty glass in front of her. "I don't know if I can do that. It sounds so much like cheating."

"So what you been doin' all this time?"

"I know that... It's just that going there and hiding out like

126

that would make it seem so much worse. I feel bad enough already having to be doing this."

"The feelin' will pass," Ruby said. "The man mi did have before meetin' Will was treatin' me the same way like Hector treat you. Well, maybe a little worse: for Robert also use to lay him hands on mi every now an' then. So naturally, mi start wonder how to leave him. At the time a wasn't doin' the little sellin' like mi doin' now, so a really didn't have any money to go anywhere. An' above all, mi so damn simple-minded: a used to think that if mi just walk outa him house an' try to make it on mi own, somethin' bad would happen to mi. Either him would come huntin' mi down, or a would die of hungry—or wild dogs would find mi sleepin' on the street an' have mi for night cap. Country girl, simple as them come."

Sharon waited silently while the other woman stared into space with an intense look on her face, taking a sip of lemonade to moisten her throat before continuing. "The abuse go on an' on, till one day mi was so fed up, achin' so much, so ashamed of miself—because him ridicule mi so much, a started thinkin' him was right: that mi really was that bad a person—a decide mi wasn' takin' any more of it. At the time, mi round the back of him house washin' some clothes. Can clearly remember some pickney out by the gate playin' football an' makin' a whole heap of noise. Robert was at work, for him use to do some tree cuttin' for one man name Mullings or Millings or somethin' like that. Him was at work an' every time mi mind would flash 'pon him. Not that a was longin' to see him but mi long to see the day when a don't have to expect to see him come home to mi. Just knowin' that he'd be home soon use to drive fear in mi heart. Fear that him go

127

come home an' start cussin' again an' find fault with everythin' a do—no matter how good mi do it. If mi cook chicken one day, him would come home, look in a the pot an' say, *'Everyday chicken, chicken! Mi soon start fly to rass! Yuh no know how fi cook nothin' else? Eeh Ruby?'* Things like that him use to find to cuss 'bout. So that day mi just make up mi mind to leave. Mi never have a clue where mi goin' or how the next meal goin' come. Him did leave some money for mi—to buy somethin' to cook dinner—an' mi never even touch it. A just wanted to leave an' mi want leave a independent woman! So mi get up from round the wash tub, throw two piece a clothes in a black plastic bag an' walk out. A didn't even take time to wash mi foot them, mi just walk out. It was like a sudden bolt of sense just hit mi an' mi start realise just how foolish a was to stay with him that long. An' when them sense hit you, you start feelin' like you don't have a second to waste—you just nuh want to waste any more time. Mi wasn' feelin' fear an' shame an' worthlessness anymore—them feelin's behind mi now. The pickney dem even stop the ball-playin' to watch mi go. All mi could feel as mi walk out a the yard like a mad woman, was freedom! A was even recitin' that Martin Luther King line them play 'pon the radio every Black History month. *Free at last, free at last, thank God almighty, I'm free at last!* An' mi say it over an' over in mi mind as a walk down Winkler Street." Ruby stopped to wipe her eyes. Sharon had never imagined that anything could bring tears to her eyes. She had always seemed so strong. Ruby then continued, "A spend four long months at Bellevue because of that man. A wait too long to leave an' when a did, it was because a lose mi mind. It was a good thing William was in the area an' see mi walkin' in the middle of the street with mi clothes trailin' out of the plastic bag. Some time later him tell mi that a was shoutin' the Martin Luther King line at the top of mi voice but a don't remember anythin' at all 'bout that. Him was the one who take mi to the hospital an' pay the bill till God help mi an' a get out." She paused to smile. "An' you know, the funny thing is that Will did like me all that time—even when a was livin' with Robert—an' him never once say anythin' till long after a come out of the hospital an' find a little job as a days worker."

"Really?"

"Yes missis. Him tell mi say him heart use to bleed them time when him see how Robert treat mi, an' how him know him would treat mi if only him did have half the chance. A must admit, mi never did like him 'cause a wasn't really interested in no man who make basket for a livin'." She laughed and looked over her shoulder as if expecting to see William standing there. But he wasn't. They could hear him whistling round the back. "But then after gettin' to know him a start get to like him an' we—you know—get together. Twelve years now an' mi have nooo regrets."

"I can see that," Sharon said.

"So what I'm takin' the whole day to try an' tell you, Sharon, is that you shouldn' wait till Hector drive you mad to make you move. Don't do anythin' drastic but don't sit around an' not do nothin' either."

"So you really think I should go be with Sugar now?" Sharon asked.

"Mi think you should a reach in him arms a'ready! You can stay with me some other time, a will make sure of that." Ruby glanced at the wooden-framed clock on the wall. "It's twenty to one. If you leave now you should get there before Hector get home. If you wait till later you might have to dodge him an' him rummy friends them an' that might not be so easy. Take you pick."

"Now?" Sharon repeated, looking at the prospects.

"Yes now! Run!" Ruby said.

With flaming cheeks and sparkling eyes, Sharon got her things from the bedroom and trotted from the house. By the time she got out to the main street she was sprinting for the first taxi in sight.

Once back in Brown's Hall she went straight to Sugar's and closed the door.

***

That evening, for the first time, Hector heard. The bed in Sugar Cane's room was squeaking like mice, but that was not loud enough to mute the erotic moans of the woman he was with. The sounds she made were like those made when fine wood was being cut by a sharp saw, *hur-hur-hur...*

Hector smiled as he wondered who had finally given the rastaman a chance. *Probably Sharlott or one of her Barn Yard Girls,* he thought. Whoever it was though, she was really enjoying herself. Either the beast was rather skilled at the art or the woman was the type that went wild for just about anything. The latter he believed was more likely the case, for a weed-smoking rastaman could never really be that good.

One thing was sure though, skilled or not, the beast had staying power. Hector had come home at about six-thirty and now it was going on the down side of seven. Between then and now there simply had been no stop to the action on the other side of the wall. And the woman seemed to know just how to boost a man's ego with what Hector considered strategic moans and squirms. Nevertheless, this was the sort of woman he often dreamed of having intercourse with. Ego boosters were also cock pleasers, he would think. They probably wouldn't make him feel so numb, like Sharon most times did.

Leaving for work the next morning, he would meet Sugar Cane who'd be checking the stand pipe for water to fill up the wash pan. "Hear you stormin' somethin' last night, dready," Hector would say, smiling in admiration.

"Yes, brother," Sugar Cane would reply as he returned the smile. "Some of that have to go on sometimes." Then he would go about his business of fetching water for Sharon to have her bath.

As he walked, Hector would just stand there for a little bit looking at the beast with humility and—to a degree—envy. He would hope that pretty soon he too would be living the life of a roaming African lion.

CHAPTER SEVENTEEN

HUR-HUR-hur-hur!

CHAPTER EIGHTEEN

CALL ME UP!

By Sugar Cane

VERSE 1:

Late last night I met a girl name Marva

She say her man no wurt a ting an' she no know wah' fi do-a.

Sometimes him good but she want somethin' weh betta.

There an' then I an' I had the answer.

CHORUS:

Call me up! Call me up!

Here's my number.

Any day! Don't delay!

If you longin' for pleasure

(Repeat chorus once)

VERSE 2:

I'm not gonna tell you I can walk on water.

But give me the chance an' I will deal with you matter.

Drown off you thirst an' devour you hunger.

Make you feel like the treasure you are.

(Chorus)

VERSE 3:

988-0167, fi Donna, Jackie, Jenny

An' the one name Gwen.

An' fi any girl weh love the nice an' nuff;

call dis yah number mek mi fill your cup, cup, cup, cup.

(Chorus)

VERSE 4:

Here's my home number...

An' one for the work place, too.

An' here's another for the cellular phone

'cause I've always got time for you girl.

CHAPTER NINETEEN

"HOW'S THAT?" Sugar Cane asked. He was seated like Buddha on the bed, wearing only an army green boxer shorts with the guitar in his lap. It was just after nine on Friday morning. The song had been written while Sharon slept. She'd gone back to Ruby's only for two nights. As she had told him, she really wasn't comfortable with the idea of hiding out like this, but right now, what she was feeling for him made the risk negligible.

Sharon shrugged. "Alright," she said. She, too, had on only her underwear and was curled up beside him like a brown cat. Last night had been as lovely as the night before and she could only feel perturbed that she wouldn't be staying with Sugar tonight, too. Hector was expecting her home from Ruby's today.

"Alright? What about great?"

"Okay, it's great."

"But?" he asked, sensing her unease.

Sharon sighed and sat up, catching his eyes. "But why are you writing this?" she asked.

Sugar Cane put the guitar aside and held her. "I'm doin' this because I an' I have plans for *us*. I just want to make some quick money so we can leave this joint. I couldn't sleep last night; I want to do all I an' I can to keep you—to make you want to run away with me as soon as possible. The two nights with you made me realise why I never wanted to go to bed at nights. I was alone there, an' sleepin' alone isn't much fun. I want to be able to sleep with you every night, Sharon. *Every night!*"

"In time, Sugar," she whispered to him, "In time–"

"But don't you feel like goin' away now?"

"Yes, yes! But not at the expense of your values. I know your songs mean much more to you than the money." She paused and then added, "And you don't have to *do* anything to keep me but remain as you are. If money was my reason, I wouldn't have slept with you in the first place, so don't let it seem that way. When it's time for you to start making a lot of money—which I believe you will—it will happen. And, yes, I will be happy when that starts happening—but I'm also happy *now*."

"So you sayin' I should put this song away an' keep tryin' with my type of songs till I make it?" he asked her.

"Yes."

"Even though this song more than likely will be accepted by the producer for good money?"

"Yes," she stressed with an air of permanence. "It's not like you're starving now, so why not wait a while longer? I believe that some day soon they'll start wanting your type of music."

Gatha would never say this, he thought. *Get the cash while you can, was more like what she would have said, after all, a*

136

little extra cash couldn't hurt much could it? The difference was clear.

"You really think so?" Sugar Cane asked.

"Yes, yes, yes." She was incessantly sincere.

"That means the sister love I an' I, then?" he asked.

Sharon thought briefly. "Taking everything into consideration, I think I do."

"I think I an' I love you too," he said.

***

That didn't stop him from taking the song to Mr. Touch, however. This he did the very next Wednesday. He didn't tell Sharon he was going, for she'd probably not want him to. But it felt like something he just had to do.

"Brilliant!" Touch exclaimed. "This is the sort of music I want you to put out. Not that *Jah-seh* shit you're always doing."

"You don't think it's too... long?" Sugar Cane asked.

"Nah man!"

"That mean you really like it?" Sugar Cane asked soberly.

"Like it? I love it! I must be honest with you, Mr. Sugar Cane, for a little while now I haven't been getting any good material, so I don't have much standing on the charts right now. But this could surely turn things around. No doubt about that."

"No doubt."

"None at all, my dear man. Already I can think of two youths who can do the singing, and this is Point-4-5's big chance to do something that can be played on the radio. More people will hear him—and being his manager you know who will benefit from that." Touch threw his head back and laughed. "Finally, Mr. Cane, we have something we can work with! Tell me how you got the inspiration; you started fucking some damn good pussy or something?"

Sugar Cane smiled. "Maybe."

"You devil you," Touch said, giving the man on the other side of the desk two thumbs up. "Just like I said. That's how the inspiration comes, man." His voice then fell to a whisper as he leaned over the desk. "Between you and me, my wife has one of the best cunts this side of town. Well, that's what my friends say when we meet for our little... group indulgence. But guess what? We haven't got that creative spark! Inspiring us is like giving a bitch brains. We can't do shit with it. But you, you're different. You've got creativity. Talent! And if it would help you to put out some more like this, I could arrange for you to be at our next party. We've known each other long enough, don't you think?"

"We have." Sugar Cane nodded.

"Good, good. I know you'd come around to seeing the light."

"Believe me, I see it alright." Sugar Cane got up with his guitar, ready to leave. "That's why I an' I came here today. I wanted to see the light. To make sure it's you and not me that's wrong."

"Wrong?" Touch asked. "What the fuck are you talking about?"

"Values."

Touch reversed the swivel chair and got out of it. He slapped

138

at an invisible mosquito on his forehead and paced the plush office space. "I don't believe this shit. What are you saying, you're not going to publish the song?"

"That's right."

"Jesus fucking Christ, man, do you know what you're saying?"

"Always," Sugar Cane said and just before leaving added, "Thanks for everythin'."

"Fuck you!" Touch shouted as Sugar Cane closed the door behind him. "I should sue you for wasting my time you damn... rent-a-dread!"

CHAPTER TWENTY

THAT WEDNESDAY was the last day of Sharon's leave and she spent it at Ruby's. They talked all day about everything and nothing, and though she had wanted to get home early she didn't manage to do so till way past seven. Time simply flew away as she related to the girls—for Grace had dropped by as well—all that had transpired over the weekend. On her way back she was a bit worried, for she was thinking Hector had come home and there was no dinner ready for him. But when she did get home she realised her worries had been unnecessary for Hector was not there. She expected him soon anyhow, so she hurried to the kitchen to start something quick. She hoped he was all right. It was not like him to get home late. Usually he would get home first and then go out if he intended to.

Sugar was on her mind too and she badly wanted to go see if he was home—but not right now. Despite everything, she still lived with Hector, and he would be coming home hungry from a hard day at the school.

While Sharon was rushing to prepare dinner, Hector was with Ken. Not over by Tony's but riding in the Volks. As they drove,

Ken would stop the car—sometimes in the middle of the road—as he called to any woman they were passing. "Hello nice lady," he would say. "Let me offer you a ride, nuh?" The women always refused, saying it was all right, or they didn't take rides from strangers, or something like that. As he drove on, if the woman in question looked particularly attractive he would say to Hector, "Damn gal sweet, eh sah?" But if she had said something offensive to him like, *"I don't talk to man who wear ears ring like them is woman. Dyam' battyman!"* he would say, "Gweh gal! Yuh nuh see how you batty flat lack-a Westmoreland ackee!" And he would move on to where they were ultimately headed. This was Sharlott's. It was Hector's idea that they went. He had simply decided that he wasn't going to let his life slip away because of one woman. He was going to go out and start having some real fun. Recapture that fire in his wire. Ken was happy, finally, Hector was coming around to realising that when something was dead it was dead. A man was made to have many women, and the only reason most of them didn't, was that their women weren't going to allow it. Truth be told, Ken thought, most men would sleep with almost any woman. It really didn't matter if the woman was pretty or not, or short or tall, or fat or skinny. All that really mattered for a man to want to sleep with a woman, was that she was indeed a clean woman (Well, some men would stretch it a lot further, but Ken wasn't prepared to go there).

Hector on the other hand wasn't quite so sure if he was really happy with the idea. Today, when he came over by Ken's desk and spoke the words, "What you say, we go up to Sharlott's later on," he could actually hear himself talking from miles away, as if he was being driven by a foreign force which he couldn't control.

It was the force of necessity, he thought. It had reached a point where he had to make a change. Either that, or his mind would explode. He had been living a lie for too long now and he simply had to move to the next phase. His days of *runnin' 'round yard* were over! It was now time to roam!

The little house was at the end of the road, quite far away from anywhere else. As they approached, all they could see of it was the yellow lantern light in its small windows.

"You come all this way every week?" Hector asked, looking out the window and seeing nothing but darkness on both sides of the road. Even above the rumble of the car's engine, he could hear the cry of millions of frogs and insects which habitated these woods.

"Religiously!" Ken said. "But it's worth it, I tell you. Every cent! Sometimes I wonder if they aren't short-changin' them-selves."

When they got to the house, a doughy-skinned woman of about fifty and no less than two hundred pounds escorted them inside. The room they entered seemed to be the biggest in the house, taking up about a half the total floor space. There were three double beds in it, arranged side by side and parted by screens that gave the look of a hospital ward. Across from those was a huge, dirty-white sofa that looked genuinely grey in the lantern light. And of course, four girls in skimpy nighties were there to greet you. The beauties girdled the men while Sharlott stood by, enjoying the picture. The room smelled of a very strong rose scented air fresh-ener which Hector thought was to mask the musty odor of stale cum and sweat. As he thought, the girls pulled off his shirt and started undoing his belt. They smelled of a talc that would have been soft if they hadn't used so much. Their warm bodies massaged his.

"Can't get this at home, Hector," Ken declared as two of the girls lead him off to the sofa where they commenced oral pleasure. "Two one time, Hector, two one time."

Hector was too overwhelmed to say anything. The two girls that remained started fondling his cock, coaxing it to hardness. They could have been dumb for none of them said anything. But they really didn't need to, for their actions and carnal eyes said it all. They were going to fuck him silly.

"Yuh look scared," Sharlott said from her post by the doorway. "Relax," she told him, "My girls will take good care of you."

He tried to relax as she suggested. Before he knew it he was on the floor and the girls were licking and caressing every inch of his body.

***

It was 2:15 a.m. when he finally got home. Sharon was up waiting. She had told herself that the hours he came in shouldn't bother her anymore, but this was a lot over the usual late appearances. As he came in, she got up from the verandah where she was talking with Sugar Cane and followed him inside.

"You could have told me you'd be late," she said, watching him walk to the bedroom and throw himself onto the bed.

"You don't own me, Sharon," Hector mumbled, exhausted. "I can go out and stay out as I fuckin' well want without havin' to say a fuckin' thing to you or anybody else". He was smiling as he spoke, still not able to get those girls out of his mind. *Those girls, those wonderful girls,* he thought. He wondered why he had not taken up on Ken's offer before.

"But Hector, I was worried sick about you. Wondering if you had been in some sort of accident or something. We all know that Ken likes to show off and gaze at women. It wouldn't be strange to think that he might just run into a wall one day while doing it."

"Don't you wish."

Now inside his room, Sugar Cane moved closer to the wall where he could hear better as they shouted at each other. Tonight, after he had told Sharon of his visit to Touch's studio, he went on to tell her that now that he'd faced up to that part of his life, the only thing that gnawed at his conscience was the thought that she wasn't his—not totally. She had kissed him then, telling him that soon enough that chapter would be completed too. As he tried to catch onto the argument he wondered if when she said *soon* she had actually meant tonight! He hoped so. He really hoped so.

"Is that what you think?" Sharon asked, coming a little closer to the bed, despising Hector even more now that he had made such a piercing statement.

"Listen woman, I'm tired. I got some real good pussy tonight and I'm dead beat. Now could you just stop your yappin' and let me get some sleep?" Hector used one foot to tear the shoe off the other. The shoes fell with a thud on the floor.

Sharon stood akimbo, her mind racing incoherently. "I said, is that what you think?"

"To call a spade a spade, yes, that is what I think. You hate the way I can go out and enjoy myself with friends and you can't 'cause you're just too fuckin' cold." He swallowed saliva and cleared his throat. "And speakin' about spades, I think you should use one to go bury that cunt of yours. It's dead."

Tears filled her eyes and no sooner than it started overflowing she went over to the dresser and began emptying the drawers of her clothes.

"What are you doin'?" Hector asked. Through his tired eyes it looked like she was just hauling things from the dresser at random to throw away. Probably even *his* things.

"What does it look like?" she asked, sounding like she had just contracted a bad case of the flu. "I'm leaving you, Hector. I think I've had enough." She spoke with forced calmness. Today she had told Ruby she was simply going to let Hector know it was over for she couldn't stand the pressure it was putting on her anymore. She had said it because the will to stop being with him had grown stronger after not being able to spend the last three nights in Sugar's arms where she truly wanted to be. She wasn't thinking of what he might do anymore. She just wanted out— and she felt that if she didn't get out, she would go crazy before the night was over. Ruby agreed with her totally, but Grace didn't. "Flow with the tide a little longer, girl," Grace had implored her. "At least till you sure where you an' Sugar goin' after you leave Hector. It won't look good to stay in the same house." And up to the point when she had come home to prepare dinner, Sharon had really consoled herself to stick with Grace's advice. But then she started talking to Sugar and was being reminded of just how much this thing was hurting him too. So she decided once again that she would have to break the news to Hector soon. If not tonight, tomorrow and if not tomorrow, the day after, but soon.

Sharon had never intended it to be like this, however. She had wanted him to come home and have dinner first—maybe even after he had returned from Tony's. She had wanted to sit him down and break it to him slowly with careful word choices. And she had even dreamed of keeping the discussion 'clean'. But even as she thought, Sharon had known that she was only fooling herself as she had just not been able to have a 'clean' discussion with Hector in a long time now.

"Leavin' me?" Hector seemed to have acquired a fresh burst of energy. "Hell, this must be my lucky night. All this time I've been wonderin' how the fuck I'm going to get rid of you and here you are, just like I never thought you would, saying you're leaving me. Things sure have a way of workin' out, don't they?" He got out of bed and came over to where she stood. Her back turned to him she resembled a mad organ player in a horror flick as she plucked things from the drawers. "Here," Hector said, "let me help you." He scooped up some of the clothes she had taken out and promptly took them outside and spilled them all on the verandah. As he did this, Sugar Cane came out to the verandah and took them all up. He put them into his room and came back to the door and waited.

When Hector took up the second bundle, Sharon grabbed onto it and he yanked it from her grip with a , *"Leeet me heeelp you!"*

Something in the bundle, quite likely an open safety pin or the hook on one of her uniforms, tore into the flesh of her right index finger.

"Fuck you!" Sharon gargled, cringing with the sting of raw nerve endings. Sharon stuck the finger in her mouth and sucked on it. The blood tasted like concentrated iron tablets.

146

This was when Sugar Cane let himself inside, ready to punch Hector but stopped in his tracks when he saw Hector offering Sharon a Band Aid for her finger. The most he could do was pull the plaster from Hector and put it on Sharon's finger himself.

"I–I'm sorry about that," Hector said, turning back to the bed. "Now get the fuck out. GO!"

After taking up the rest of her clothes, Sugar Cane escorted her home.

CHAPTER TWENTY-ONE

TO SHARON, everything seemed so unreal. It was as if she were in a terrible dream that was going on for too long now. However long though, dreams had a definite end; but what her heart desired was a steady relationship with a man who loved her. Time after time, men with worldly possessions would come offering her a better life not knowing that if she were a sucker for social standing she would have stayed home with her parents and followed the path her father had paved for her. It was comforting to know she had a safety net of having her parents' wealth available to her, if necessary. She wanted the simple life: the chance to grow into who she wanted to be. And also to be loved. There was no guarantee that any of those other men would truly love her, for in this world hardly anybody really loved anybody. So, if somebody truly loved you, it was a treasure you didn't want to give up for anything at all. And the fact that deep down, she had wondered whether she truly loved Hector didn't matter seriously, for she always believed she could *learn*.

Unfortunately, what she hadn't thought of then, was that there was no guarantee that Hector's true love for her would continue indefinitely. Strangely enough, this wasn't why she was crying now, even as Sugar Cane tried to comfort her.

What Sharon Gordon wept for was the five years she had wasted with a man she never loved! A man who captured her mind with kindness—then killed it slowly with neglect and verbal abuse. Now she was mad at herself for not having left him a long time ago, instead of thinking any day now things would change to how they used to be. *No guarantee*, her mind echoed. None with Hector, Sugar Cane, nor anybody else for that matter. *No guarantee*—she had learned this the hard way. It was cold and harsh, but that was life. You were lucky not just if you found love but if this love stayed around forever. This was what most people who ever sought love secretly desired. Love that stuck around.

Was Sugar's love going to stick around for her? Sharon didn't know this. Was hers going to stick around for him? She didn't know that either. It didn't matter anyway, for they both loved each other tonight. And if five years from now he too decided to leave her, it would surely hurt, and she would surely cry, but at least she wouldn't feel so *fucking stupid!* She loved him too, and that made all the difference. Mutual love and respect were never a waste of time, but spending years attempting to achieve this might very well be.

This was no dream, it was the real world and it wasn't going to end just yet. She would be crying for the rest of tonight and maybe all of tomorrow as well. But she could console herself with the thought that when she did stop crying, that part of her life would be over and a new chapter would begin.

CHAPTER TWENTY-TWO

UNTIL HE saw it happening, Hector had never once thought that Sugar Cane was actually going to have Sharon staying with him. Sugar Cane and Sharon were close friends, Hector knew this. So he could understand the dreadlocks putting her up for a day or two after he had thrown her out—but what he now witnessed was... *absurd*. A week went by and Sharon was still there. And many times while he sat on his bed eating the terrible dinner he'd rigged up for himself, he could smell the meal she was preparing over there. Meals, that just last week she would have been preparing with him in mind.

But what jolted him most was what he heard tonight for the second time. *Hur-hur-hur...*

Only this time, he knew very well who it was that opened her legs for the beast. And it all dawned on him now, that while she was with him she had this animal fucking her. Maybe she was the real reason Sugar Cane came to Brown's Hall: they'd had a long distance affair going on and couldn't stand it anymore so he came a little closer. It was also possible that she had slept with quite a few men here in Brown's Hall. *Maybe even Ken!... Fuckin' slut!*

he thought. All along I was so stupid to think that she wouldn't do that sort of thing to me, that she was the old-fashioned kind of girl. Shit! Was I wrong. She's just like the Barn Yard Girls. He tried not to let this bother him however, for he too was starting a new chapter in his life. One in which Sharlott's girls and junk food played an integral role. Made absolutely no sense worrying about what a bitch Sharon was at this stage for it wasn't worth it. She was out of his life for good. He didn't even acknowledge her presence whenever they passed each other in the yard, and likewise she didn't see him either. It was like malice between two children.

As for Sugar Cane, Hector literally didn't see him at all. He didn't know if he was hiding or what, but he just didn't leave his room anymore—at least, not when Hector was around to see him if he did. The only sign of him was his laugh and erotic moans as he and Sharon apparently had a ball in his den. But Hector didn't envy them for Hector knew better.

For instance, he knew that Sharon was a fucking mule, and when Sugar Cane found this out, all the fun would cease. Those primitive type of men loved to have quite a few little... *picknies* making noise in their homes and they didn't think too much of adoption. She'd probably try to deny it to Sugar Cane too, but just like he had, the beast would find out, and that would only make matters worse.

But then, Hector was smart. He wasn't so sure he could say the same about Sugar Cane. When Sharon had come home with that phony doctor's certificate saying she was quite fertile, he had been keen enough to figure this out. The weed-smoker might not be.

Smart or not though, he had to agree that Sugar Cane did get him with that wild beast act. *I an' I is a African at heart,* he could remember Sugar Cane professing that night while they chatted on the verandah, *the one-woman thing can't hold me... I an' I want to roam like a lion.* Good thing he hadn't mentioned this to the guys at the bar, or they just wouldn't stop the guffaw. Especially if he had told them that he actually found some respect for the beast because of this, when all along the rastaman was plotting to grab his woman the moment he let her go.

"We warn you 'bout that man, Hector," was all Ken managed to say now. "We told you that that rastaman might just fuck your woman from under you and look now: prophesy come to pass. If you have a big, trang, horny man walkin' round the yard every day with nothin' to do but play guitar to you woman this sort of thing bound to happen." As usual with them this was said in jest and they all took it as such. That was all. Except Hector, who laughed outwardly, knew within himself that prophesy had indeed come to pass. All they knew was that he threw Sharon out and the rastaman took her up like a junk truck—and this was all they were going to know for sure. Anything else would be considered bar jokes and town gossip, no matter how close to the truth they really were. Hector could live with this.

"What can I say?" Hector said and shrugged. "The dread came like a fuckin' blessin' and took my burden away."

"I hope you keep thinkin' that way for your own good," Floyd said from over his beer. It was after ten p.m. There was no music playing on the jukebox, the TV was off and the bar empty excepting the three regulars and Tony. When they spoke their voices carried like ghosts on the sharp wind that whirled through the empty cross roads.

"Whatever could make me stop?" Hector asked.

Floyd smiled. "I don't know... maybe you start wantin' her back."

This was when Ken swayed over to Hector and patted him on the back. "Hector's havin' far too much fun to even think of goin' back there, and I can personally vouch for that. Ain't no cunt like cunt for cash, eh Hector?"

"Damn right," Hector answered and drank to it.

"What's so special about whores?" Floyd asked, having the last of his beer. Tony was going to supply him with another but Floyd gave him the stop sign. He'd had enough for tonight.

"They don't whine," Ken answered, "they wind."

"Ken, you're so wretched," Floyd said at this. "Is that all you can think of a woman as... a sex object?"

Ken shrugged. "No. But it's a start," he then said and started laughing, spittle sprinkling from his mouth.

"That's what I'd call a good fuckin' start," Hector contributed with a smart-ass grin on his face.

"And Hector, you followin' his lead! You who should know better." Floyd shook his head in distress. "You who had a damn good woman in your life. You know how much man would give arm and leg to have a woman like Sharon?"

"You may be right but hey! What the fuck that have to do with me?"

"It have everythin' to do with you," Floyd said.

"I beg to disagree," Ken interrupted. "Hector is his own man and if he feels the girl's a bitch, he has a right to his opinion."

153

"I'm not sayin' she's a bitch," Hector said.

Ken caught his eyes. "What the fuck are you sayin' then, Hec?"

"I'm just sayin' she's not worth my arm and leg, that's all." Even though he was no longer with her he was finding that he couldn't deal with slaughtering her like this—even if he did think she was a bitch and a half. "If some other guy want to: fine—but that's not me."

"Not anymore," Floyd said. Tony had his back turned to the conversation as he washed the used glasses. He could see them from the mirror that centered the shelves of liquor bottles so he really wasn't missing too much of the drama.

"What's that supposed to mean?" Hector asked.

"Just what I said, not anymore. I can remember when you and Sharon just started livin' up here, you didn't even want to sit with us for one beer. You had to go home to see her. And every other word you mentioned her name. We all used to sit here and laugh 'bout how much you was pussy-whipped—but you never let that get to you, for you knew that being pussy-whipped isn't such a bad thing. Back then you used to think the world of her cookin'— you even came by here one evenin' with a sample of her stew peas for me to taste, remember? *Can't keep this to myself—God will sin me,* was what you said. And I must admit, the stewpeas was really good, I can still remember it and that was donkey years ago. Only you get it so much you lost the taste for it—or maybe you just take it for granted that everybody's stewpeas taste just as good, so this was really nothing special. But I can bet you it still just as good—or better now. Only it's not yours anymore, is it? You dash it weh like a fool."

Ken got to his feet applauding. "Now *that's* what I call a damn good speech. Just Cop done it again." His clapping hands sounded like fire crackers going off in the hush of the night.

Hector chuckled but didn't laugh. He glanced across at the quiet juke and then got up. "Gentlemen," he said, "I think this is it for me for tonight." After which he turned and walked away.

CHAPTER TWENTY-THREE

TWO WEEKS passed. *Floyd was right,* Hector thought. The more he came home and not finding Sharon there, the more he wondered if he had made the right decision after all. It wasn't like she had gone to spend time with Ruby and he would expect her home at the end of the stay. She was gone. For good. He had chased her away.

The memories were coming back now. The good ones. The memories Floyd had jogged that night at Tony's. And he was forced to wonder just how did he manage to stop remembering all these things. It was a lot like breathing, he thought. You did it so often and it all seemed to come so naturally, you sometimes forgot it kept you going till one day, you find yourself trapped under the rubble left by an earthquake and you start thinking, *Fuck! Pretty soon the air's goin' to run out and I'm goin' to suffocate under here like the mortal I am.* And you start remembering just how important breathing was, and you also start thinking, if you got out okay, you were going to give up smoking and buy only ozone friendly products—for this breathing thing was serious shit. Yes sir, sometimes it took a little suffocating to remember just how important to your living breathing really was.

But this would pass, he thought with much optimism. It was like the ghost pains you felt after losing a limb. It was only normal that you felt a little lonely coming home everyday to an empty home when for the most part of five years it had been otherwise.

He genuinely missed the dinner though. Smelling it these days and not being able to taste it, was becoming like torture. For this reason, he sometimes deliberately stayed away till he was certain they were done eating over there. But in time, he knew, and with a little self-discipline, he would get over this too. What made it a little more manageable too, was that she wasn't always there. She stayed with the beast maybe three or four days of the week then went away. He would figure it was up by Ruby's that she went at these times.

Today, Ken took him to Spanish Town where they visited what Ken called *another fuck shop*. Ken was all excited about the whole thing, but as far as Hector was concerned, you've seen one hooker joint, you've seen them all. The girls were good, but then, this was their job. And besides, it was beginning to be an expensive habit to keep doing on a weekly basis. It was probably cheaper to pick up one-night-stands at night clubs, he thought, but this was another whole field for him.

Since being out on his beastly trail, he had learned one vital lesson: no matter how the movies made it seem, without a steady girl in your life, free pussy was just not the easiest thing to get. You had to do some serious begging for some of that. Especially so for a guy who wasn't extraordinarily skilled with the ladies or particularly good-looking. If you really worked at it, you could end up getting a girl into a sleazy motel room for an hour or so, but those girls most times weren't worth the effort. The good ones didn't find beer guts and being gruff attractive.

Of course, while Hector felt like this, Ken was the direct opposite, for he got girls leaving the clubs with him after a few minutes of conversation. The only time Hector can remember a girl saying no to Ken, was when Ken suggested to the girl that his friend would like to check her out.

So Hector started an exercise programme. Every morning he would jog a little and do ten or so push-ups before going off to work. And he thought, *Sharon tolerated me with my beer gut so why can't they? Too fuckin' stuck-up! That's what they are.*

The exercises were really draining him, so instead of going into Spanish Town with Ken (who just never seemed to be out of energy) that Friday, Hector decided to go home early. As he turned the key in his door to go inside, he saw Sharon only just coming into the yard. She carried a black plastic shopping bag in one hand, as if she were coming from the grocery with goodies for the rastaman. He stopped right there, the door ajar and the key still in it. It had been almost a week now since he had seen her at all, and it had seemed more like five years. She wore a just-above-the-knees summer dress that was held to her shoulders by what resembled bikini strings. It flowed sensually about her with every bounce. Hector swallowed hard and wiped his sweating palms on his pants, swinging his texts and chalk box from one hand to the next as he did this.

When Sharon saw him eyeing her, her strides slowed to a stroll. She wasn't sure what to think, as she started on the verandah. There was still enough rage inside her to make her want to use the bag she held and clout him hard for just standing there—

but there was something else that would have prevented her even if she was really going to do it. *Pity.* Hector had lost weight—lots of weight—but not from his gut. The pants he wore, sagged as if he had shit in them, and the bones of his cheeks, elbows and hands seemed excessively pronounced. And he badly needed a shave.

"Hi, Sharon," Hector said.

"Hi," she said back. It was the first time since breaking up and it felt rather unnatural.

"How's it goin'?" he asked and found himself swaying a little. Her skin was so smooth, he thought, and her cleavage kept forcing his eyes to look. *Look at me,* it said to him, *loooook at me!*

"Okay, I guess," she replied. Actually she was doing great. She didn't like the idea of having to be staying between Sugar's and Ruby's because she hadn't found a place to rent as yet; but Sugar Cane was just so wonderful to her: there was just no room to feel down even if she had reason to. He helped with the cooking, dusting, and went with her to the market whenever he found the time to. This was how Ruby and Grace finally got the chance to meet the man they both lobbied for. They were more than pleased with what they saw. The washing was done mostly by Mrs. Bailey who now came on Wednesdays to wash for them. The weekends were still reserved for Hector's laundry.

"I see you've been... *exercising,*" Sharon then said to Hector to avoid the uncomfortable brooding silence.

She's been watchin' me, Hector thought, *she's been watchin' me sweat as I flex my muscles in the mornin's. I bet she's beginnin' to want me back.* "Yes," he then said, trying to pull in his stomach, "I've been trying to stay in shape for the world out there. It's a jungle, I tell you..."

He badly needs some taking care of, she thought, *his eyes are so sunken.* "That's good... that's good."

"Yeah, it's been great." He breathed deeply.

"Okay then," Sharon said and started off. "Take care."

"–Sure, sure...always." He felt himself sway again and he stuffed his free hand in his pocket. Her ass was so tight, and her legs so beautiful—he wondered why they never looked like this when she was his. *They always looked like this,* a voice told him, *it's just that you stopped seein' them.*

"Sharon!" he called just before she turned the corner that took the verandah all the way to the other man's door.

"Yes," she said, stopping in her tracks.

"I–ah...I'm sayin' that..." He wanted to tell her he was sorry and he wouldn't mind if they talked sometimes, if only for a few minutes. But then he thought, *no; she might think I'm suckin' up to her when I'm not. I won't say I'll never do it but not now... let her suffer some more.* "You take care, too," he ended.

She smiled. "I will," she said and turned away.

He went inside and tried to sleep, but couldn't. So he got up and went over to Tony's where he ordered a beer and sipped at it alone till Floyd came along two hours later.

CHAPTER TWENTY-FOUR

"SHARON!" SUGAR Cane called as he started into the yard. He was excited. "Sharon!" He walked briskly as if he wanted very badly to use the bathroom.

The door came open. Sharon was standing there, the light from the room giving her silhouette a glowing edge. It was after 11 p.m. but she hadn't been sleeping for she'd decided that tonight was a night that she just had to wait up, no matter how late he came in.

When Sugar Cane got to the door he pulled her close and kissed her. She felt enticingly warm as he held her against the night air. "Guess what, baby?" he asked, eyes as fervent as those of a child who has just been let loose in the world's largest toy store. "I've got somewhere for us to live!'

"Really?"

"Yes! Jah-Jah Son has this friend who was sellin' him house and Jah-Jah-Son want me to live there."

"But Sugar, we can't afford a house," she reminded him.

"That's exactly what I an' I tell him and he said, *'I know that.*

That's why I an' I goin' buy it and subtract the sum from the money I goin' make when I an' I start producin' you'."

"Producing you? He's going to produce your songs?"

"Yes, baby, yes!" He scooped her up and took her inside, heeling the door shut behind them. A single lit candle was at the center of the table and dinner was there waiting, buffet style. Steamed fish, rice, cooked vegetables and green peas. The sight was a shock to his eyes. He laid her on the bed and for a time was struck with humility. He had expected dinner, yes, but nothing like this.

"I have something to tell you, too," she said and beckoned him to come closer.

Sugar Cane sat down on the bed beside her and held onto the hand that she reached out to him.

"Sugar, I'm pregnant," she said.

His eyes went wide and it wasn't quite clear whether he was happy or not. "Pregnant???... Are you sure?" His eyes automatically went to her tummy.

"Of course I'm sure. Did the test at the clinic this morning," she said and watched his face very carefully. Men could be a strange set when it came on to the topic of pregnancy. Even some of the most sedate guys went berserk when the *p*-word hit them.

Sugar Cane's expressionless face melted into a smile which widened to a toothy grin. "Selassie Jah!" he shouted and leaped from the bed. *Things were really workin' out,* he thought, his God had not forgotten him after all. He pulled off his tam and flashed his locks about his face. "Rastafari!" He invited Sharon to come dance with him as he shouted in jubilation. "Blessed!

Blesss-ed! BLESSSEEEEEED!!!"

Over by Tony's Hector heard the commotion and wondered what the fuck was that all about.

CHAPTER TWENTY-FIVE

IT WAS the following morning that Sharon and Sugar Cane left Brown's Hall. They had stayed up an hour and a half after celebrating the pregnancy and talked about what they were going to do.

"I want to leave this place right now," Sugar Cane had said. "It's bad enough I an' I youth get conceived under a rented roof, but that child not goin' to develop any further under one as long as I can help it."

"You're talking as if you're the only one in this thing," Sharon had told him. "What about me? Don't I have a say?"

"I'm sorry, baby. We really should leave this place soon now that we have the chance, don't you think?"

"That's more like it. I'm ready to leave this place whenever you are. But you know I'm keeping my job at the clinic?"

"As long as you livin' with me, where you want to work is up to you. All I an' I need to know is that you are beside me at night." That settled it. Sugar Cane got up at dawn to secure a taxi and by six he was back with Samuel Sheggs.

It was the rumble of the engine coming in that alerted Hector that something was going on. He was just coming from the shower and had only managed to get his boxers on. He had not slept well last night either for the sounds that kept droning from next-door had started affecting him in a chronic way. There were times when he felt like screaming his head off when her heard Sharon's cries of pleasure as the dreadlocks drove himself into her. There were times when he wanted to get out of bed and go tear Sugar Cane's door off and take his woman back. But then he thought, the feelings would pass, and he'd be fine. And besides, he knew better than to take him on. It was like a recovering drug addict, there were times when you felt like you'd die if you didn't get a fix and you'd probably do anything to get one. But if you remained strong the urge would pass and you'd feel better about yourself at the end of the day. It was the very same principle.

No, it wasn't, he thought and went to the living room where he looked out the window. A Nissan Sunny cab was parked just in front of the verandah, its roof still dotted with dew and the windscreen smoky with condensed water. The driver was a short man of about fifty, wearing a tweed cap and dark blue sweater. Hector had seen him before but didn't know his name. He was briskly using a yellow rag to clear the windscreen. Sugar Cane came into view. He was carrying a bulging tote bag and his guitar slung across his back. The bag went into the trunk while the guitar was placed on the cab's rear seat.

Hector brought his hands to his face and closed his eyes. They were leaving, he thought. *Sharon is leavin' Brown's Hall.* Was he prepared for this? He didn't think so. He didn't think so at all.

Hector paced up and down the floor several times in his usual

165

way as he tried to get his thoughts in order. There were two distinct voices in his head at this point, one that wanted Sharon back and one that was too macho to admit it. *Fuck pride and go beg her to come back,* Hector number one was pleading. *Let's face it, you aren't exactly doin' great without her. Look at you for Christ's sake. You look like shit!*

Don't listen to him, Hector number two told him, *don't listen to that chicken shit. All you need to do is be cool, man, for nothin' beats that shit, you hear me? Nothin'!!!*

"Feel like such a fool," he murmured. If he were a smoker he would have cleared a twenty-pack since hearing the cab. "I played the ass and now she's leavin'—for good!"

But she's not gone yet, Number One said. *She might be leavin' but she's not gone yet.*

"Are you sayin' there's still... *hope*?" Hector asked himself.

There's still hope... there's always still hope.

Fuck that! Number Two exclaimed. *The bitch is a hopeless bore and the farther she goes the better for all of us–*

"–Don't call her bitch!"

Wha??? Man, we go way back, Number Two said, *I know what's good for us. Hey! Where're you goin'? Hector don't be a fool, man, Hector!*

He didn't waste any more time to get clothes on. Hector ran out on the verandah, his eyes sweeping the entire area for Sharon. So intense was his gaze that he just didn't see the car at all and wondered if they had left while he was arguing with himself. But then the cab came into view, the driver staring at him with fear in his eyes. *Must think I've gone mad,* Hector thought. Not long after, Sharon came round the corner of the verandah. She had two brown leather travelling bags in her hands. Sugar Cane walked beside her with a loaded dish drainer.

"Sharon, I must talk to you," Hector said with much urgency.

For a little while they both stood there looking at him, not quite knowing what to think. Then Sharon rested both bags on the verandah and stepped forward. "I'll be fine," she told Sugar Cane who stepped after her with great concern. To prevent Hector anymore embarrassment, she followed him inside and closed the door.

Hector walked to and fro, nervously running his hand through his hair and wiping his face. "You must think I've gone nuts, right?" he asked and looked out the window like a fugitive. Just as he thought, the cab was still there—*waiting*.

Sharon didn't answer. The engine of the cab came alive, which meant Sugar Cane had finished packing in everything and was ready to pull out. It was revved twice and then left to idle.

"Would you come back to me if I asked you to?" Hector was standing in front of her now, so close she could smell the toothpaste on his breath, his hollow eyes never leaving hers. "I mean, I've really learned my lesson. I'm no good without you. *God!* I don't know what I was thinkin' all those times I was neglectin' you and saying' all those things. It is like I'd gone crazy—but I'm sane now. And...and if you give me another chance, I promise things'll be different. Just give me another chance, Sharon, just one more."

"Hector, I can't," she said mildly.

"But you can," he insisted timidly. "There has to be a soft

spot in your heart to forgive me. Think of all the good times we shared together, we could have them again." He reached out and pulled her closer to him, staring miles into her brown eyes. "Just don't leave me this way. *Don't.*"

She looked at his hands and he let go of her. "Sorry, 'bout that," he said and stepped back one pace. "Guess I have no right holdin' another man's woman like that, do I?"

Tears came into her eyes and she didn't try to hold them back. She used the heel of one hand to wipe her eyes.

"Tell them to go on and leave you," Hector said. "He can survive without you, I can't. I've tried."

Sharon came over to where he stood and hugged him tightly. Her tears wetted his neck and her fingers pressed hard against his bare back. She was actually feeling guilty for what had happened to them, maybe there was something she could have done to make him realize what was happening to them before it got to this. His arms tightened around her and for a moment she thought she could feel his hardness.

"I can't," Sharon affirmed and slowly pulled away. She shook her head. "I can't." And when she said it, she wasn't thinking that she was already pregnant for another man. And she wasn't thinking about all the wrong Hector had done her either. All that ran through Sharon's mind was that she just didn't love this man. That's why things had gotten to this: he had started slipping and she didn't love him enough to let him see.

Sharon ran from the room and into the waiting cab. "Drive away," she said, "quick!" She then buried her face on Sugar Cane's chest and cried as the car pulled out of the yard and started out for

Spanish Town. Sugar Cane didn't ask what was wrong, for in an intuitive kind of way, he knew.

After about a mile and a half, Sharon raised her face to the fresh breeze that slapped her as the cab sliced its way through the crisp of morning.

"Okay?" Sugar Cane asked and kissed her on the forehead.

"I think so," she said, looking out at the green mountain range that seemed to encircle them. By this time, she was eagerly wanting to arrive at their new home. She was even thinking what new curtains she would be getting for the windows, and the decor for the baby's room. She took the rainbow-coloured bracelet from her handbag and put it on her wrist. "Sugar, tell me about Rastafari," she said.

He chuckled and held her close. The cab just passed the sign that read, *SPANISH TOWN, 26 KM AHEAD*. "Rastafari sweet, baby, sweet like sugarcane."

Afterword

8:45 p.m.

2.04.01

Writing a novel is a lonely job. Usually the writer sits in solitude at the word processor for endless hours trying for the life of him to tell a story he hopes the reader will enjoy. Nevertheless, he never truly does it alone. He gets help. Lots of it. Sometimes more than his lazy ass deserves because people around him actually believe in what he is doing.

This said, I would like to acknowledge Tracy Evans for rewriting the manuscript when I was just feeling too disillusioned to do it myself. At that time, paying someone to get it done would have been a pretty steep climb while someone offering to do it for free, nothing short of a miracle. That miracle happened. You. Thanks.

Alex Morgan

Printed in the United States
200079BV00006B/601-630/A